COUNTING
WOLVES

Michael F. Stewart

Chapter 1

The wolf hunts.

It prowls as I hurry down the hall past teenagers scavenging for pencils and kisses. Locker doors slam and laughter sprays like gunshots, but I ignore the jibes. I've bigger things to worry about. Like the wolf. Like the fire door. It's a door in the middle of the hallway. For me, that door might as well be a bank of thorns. It might as well be a dragon's hellish maw. But the wolf hunts, and through that door is my only escape.

I start to count. This is the important part. I have to count right. Not too fast, nor too slow. All the way to one hundred. It must be spoken aloud, without interruption. Whispering is acceptable; the count keeps my wolf to the Dark Wood. It keeps me on safety's slender path.

Seventeen, eighteen, nineteen . . .

Stephanie, a pert blonde whose butt I used to kick on the basketball court, leans against the doorframe and raises an eyebrow. "I love this next bit," she says, pulling her phone out and holding it like a magic wand. "This is Steph Lattersby reporting from Hopedell High School. What you are about to witness is the magical thinking of fifteen-year-old Milly Malone, as she prepares to leap over whatever chasm she is presently hallucinating."

It's no chasm. My mother told the story best.

There once was a girl who was the wolf's coveted meal. Every day she would wake to the wolf huffing and puffing at her door, and every night it would hunt the girl in her dreams. Then one day she learned a magic spell. If she counted to one hundred before going through doors, eating meals, and any speech, she could banish the wolf to the Dark Wood and survive in the world as long as she stayed on the clear path. But, each day, the wolf grew hungrier, waiting for her to step off the trail, and for her spell to break . . .

That's what I fear the most. That one day my magic count won't work.

My mouth dries as I whisper, and I struggle to keep the count slow and steady. Forty-two, forty-three, forty-four . . . but my wolf has crept behind me and bent its head low. Yellow eyes burrow into my spine. The gray wolf, mountainous, savage, and unrelenting.

"This could take a while, folks," Stephanie says in a deep, queenly voice. "You'll have to wait like everyone else does here for this very *special* princess."

Sixty-six, sixty-seven . . . Other students stop to see what Stephanie records—scavengers after my bones. Some, having figured out that it's me, roll their eyes and move on, but the rest—most of them—fold their arms and wait with Stephanie, lips lifted to show teeth, eyes as bright as the wolf's.

Hot breath blows rank and moist on hands I hold tight to my thighs.

I can run, but that would be into the Dark Wood, and from its shadows I might never return.

Seventy-seven, seventy-eight . . . I tense, ready for paws to clamp down on my shoulders, for claws to sink into my bony chest. It's so strong. I can't keep it back much longer.

"I think she said eighty-nine. Get ready—here comes the magic." Stephanie's voice lifts. "This is going to be fabulous! Stupendous!"

The students begin to clap with my counting, but they're not on beat. Their poor timing makes it more difficult. Tears stream down my cheeks. If only they could hear me screaming inside, if they understood that I did this for them. The wood looms at the edges of my vision, branches entwining and bearing down, groping.

Something swipes at my shoulder. I shout the remaining count. "Ninety-eight, ninety-nine, one hundred!"

I clench my hands and eyes, bend at the knee, and hop through the doors.

The cheer is half cackle. "See, what did I tell you? Wasn't that amazing?" Stephanie continues, but I don't care. The woods have fallen away. I draw deep cleansing breaths. The hall shines with summery fluorescent light. My fingers probe my shoulder for the claw marks. *Nothing.* I beat the wolf back—for now. I wipe tears with the sleeve of my sweater. At least Billy wasn't here for this one.

The students drift off, headed for classes. While I gather myself, I avoid eye contact with those who remain and read the poster on the door.

Dance, Dance, Dance! Have a monster ball! It's for this

Friday—Halloween. I want to go to the ball. For someone who has to count to speak or enter through doorways, a date limited to one room and virtually no talking is a Cinderella story.

"Hey, what class you got next?" There's Bill. I turn to him and wrap my arms around his thin waist, counting as fast as I can. "It's okay, Mill. Can't be that bad a class."

He's smiling down at me, making the usual banter while he waits for me to finish my count. He checks over his shoulder where a retinue of other jocks linger. I count louder, so Bill knows how far along I am. "Seventy-two, seventy-three . . ." Then I go back to whispering, which is faster.

His tennis partner sighs, but Billy shuts him up with a glare. "Hey, I don't make fun of you for avoiding cracks."

His partner shrugs.

. . . ninety-eight, ninety-nine, one hundred. I'm gripping Bill's shoulders, staring up into brown eyes, tight curly hair, and a cut jaw. I'm done and I say in a rush, "Is there blood on my back?"

"Blood?" He pulls me around. "No . . . are you all right?"

Waving off what I'd asked as if I was kidding, I pull out my phone and tap out a note—I can't speak again unless I count to a hundred once more.

LOL, I have Phys Ed. I try to smile, but something hit me— the wolf got me. It's never struck me before. It's stronger. I rake my fingernails from my shoulder to the small of my back and then type. *You've got Calculus, please let's trade?* It's a joke, but the plea on my face suggests otherwise. I'd trade if I could, but he's a grade older. *I'd better get going.*

"Yeah, hop to it," he says. It's a cruel jab, but the accompanying wink takes away the sting.

I head for the change room, three more doors, five if I change in a stall. My wolf knows I'm alone again. It watches. The halls have emptied of students, which helps with the next doorway, but I enter to a room filled with girls, most of whom are already geared up and punching through the two doors between the showers and the gym. I hate those doors. A double set that snare me for a hundred count between them. I count and then spin my locker combo, sagging against the cool steel when I get it right the first time.

I pull my sweater over my head. And I ignore the glances. My ribs stick out more than I'd like, but I don't have an eating disorder, I just don't eat much. I have to count to take a bite *and* chew, so even if I could bear the stares, I wouldn't be able to finish much of the lunches my stepmom packs me. Besides, the food is likely filled with slow-acting poisons.

Before pulling on my gym clothes, I shuffle to the mirror. My green eyes are haunted, and when I search for claw marks it's not only my ribs that stick out, but the wings of my shoulder blades. Four long welts trace down my back, not enough to break the skin. Almost like a warning. Gooseflesh bubbles up along my arms. My spell weakens. If it breaks, all the denizens of the Dark Wood will roam free. Everyone's wolves.

I sit back on the bench, forget what I was doing for a minute, and then realize that I'm not wearing any socks. Malnourishment does nothing good for my brain. I pull on a fresh pair, then my shoes, which takes longer than it should. By the time I'm done, the change room has cleared, which will mean push-ups from the coach. I turn toward the gym doors and shudder, trying to steel myself.

The showerheads dribble; even the ceiling drips moisture as I shuffle beneath. The humid air cloys at me. I taste mold. Before the first door, I begin my count. My whispering echoes against the slick tiles, hissing back. My wolf hears. I lift my voice to cover the smacking of its jaws. Alone, in a change room, weaponless. I am prey.

Forty-four, forty-five . . . The huffs from its throat are like laughter. I don't want to look. It wants nothing more than to chew on me and gnaw the gristle from my bones.

. . . one hundred. I straight-arm the door as I hop through, falling back against it, hearing the rasp of claws across the metal. But there's no rest; I'm trapped. A door before me and a door behind me. I start the count again. The wolf can reach anywhere. There's nowhere near enough room in here for us both. If the cavernous shower felt claustrophobic, this in-between place is a coffin.

Eight, nine, ten . . . Claws sweep under the door. I leap from them, landing against the second door to the gym and tripping over a shoelace. The door swings. I fall across the threshold, staring up at the bright, silver lights blazing overhead. For a moment I keep counting, but it's too late for that. My wolf roars. There's no option left but the woods.

"Milly?" the coach shouts, but I've missed my count. My heart struggles to clamber out between my ribs. Sweat erupts from my flesh. Night rushes in from the sides of my vision. Twigs snatch at my arms. Bark scrapes over me as I'm carried like I'm crowd-surfing the treetops, deeper and darker into my nightmare. Lost in the blackest of fairy tales.

Chapter 2

"Romila Malone, are you Romila Malone?" The nurse in blue scrubs spattered with something I really don't want identified is waving me through from the far side of the emergency room doorway.

"Hurry, Milly, she's calling us," says my stepmother, Adriana.

But I'm rooted on this side of the door until I complete my count. A fresh wave of fear starts in my groin, swells in my stomach, and roars into my lungs. This place is a wolf den. A warren of doors and questions requiring answers.

One, two, three . . . An ambulance brought me to the hospital, but from there Adriana took over.

"She counts," Adriana says to the nurse. "It's something she does."

Yeah, it's my thing.

"You the mom?" the nurse asks.

"Yes . . . stepmom. Sorry about all this."

I've warned my father about this woman. Adriana's very clever. My real mom loved to use fables and fairy tales to teach me important lessons. You know, like don't go off the path,

Little Red Riding Hood, or the Big Bad Wolf will get you, and rape you, and devour you. Every night my mother read from a tome of them—my book of tales.

Well, she warned me about the wolf that was chased away from a flock of sheep by watchful dogs until the wolf found a fleece. Being a smart wolf, she laid the fleece on her back and, pretending to be a sheep, faked out the dogs, leading the lambs into the Dark Wood where she tore them into bloody strips. That's Adriana with her carefully applied makeup, her clothes that hide what she wants to hide and push up what she wants in your face. She's an imposter. I just can't trust her.

"She has to count to a hundred before going through doorways," Adriana explains to the nurse.

Why is it always the damn stepmother? The evil stepmother who betrays me and Snow White and poor Gretel—and who won't let me leave the ER. And all these doors.

As I finish my count I know the wolf has darted ahead and I must follow. With my hand on Adriana's shoulder, I close my eyes, tense, and hop through the doorway.

"Right in here," the nurse says. She directs me into a large ward and sits me on a too-hard bed. I reel from the scent of butchery. But Adriana only smiles, wipes a blue plastic chair down with a wet-wipe and then sits. We're in an open area with maybe eight beds, but it's tough to see exactly how many due to all the screens. Machines rustle and chitter like hidden animals. I whiff vomit too. Someone's crying. This is the last place on earth anyone wants to be. A clock ticks on the wall. It'll be dark soon.

It's been almost four hours since the ambulance brought me

from the school. Most of that time was spent waiting in the emergency room. After the sirens, and lights, and blown-through intersections, I hit the ER, where the wolf attack didn't rate as high as the chest pain, the knife wound, or the girl with the swollen tongue. So I waited with my stepmom. At least I beat out sniffles kid and broken-finger guy.

Today was a bad day. I'd eaten my toast this morning. Drank my milk. Half a cup of it. More than enough for the day. More than enough to survive. It's the wolf that's growing stronger. Places like this are what it likes best. Everywhere trees. Everywhere traps.

"I haven't told your father yet," Adriana says. I shake my head and point to my chest. "I'm fine with you calling him first, so long as there are no decisions to make."

I nod.

Across from my bed a Goth kid hunkers in a shadowy cloak. He stares out through black-rimmed eyes as bleak and putrid as swamp water. Black hair cascades from a part in the middle of his forehead. He stares. At the jar of cotton swabs? The clock? No, it's gotta be knife-wound guy, who is in the midst of getting a Frankenstein row of stitches across his bicep.

"Hi, I'm Doctor Sachay, what seems to be the problem?" The doctor's reading a chart as she asks the question. I shudder and don't bother counting.

"Milly collapsed during gym class," Adriana says.

The doctor sighs and looks up. "Uh-huh, pushing yourself, were you?" She reaches down, touches cool fingertips to my wrist and checks my pulse.

Adriana's breath hitches mid-sob. "No, you don't understand. She's not eating. Look how skinny she is. She needs a doctor. She won't eat. At home it's even worse, she won't do anything—she can't, because she has to count."

It's not true. Home is my sanctuary; there I don't have to speak or move between rooms like when I'm at school. It's Adriana who makes it hell, prodding me from couch to kitchen, kitchen to desk, and desk to bed. Do this. Do that. You missed a spot in your sweeping. Once I caught her moving the furniture to prove herself right.

Blood pressure is next. "When was your last meal, Milly?" the doctor asks. "What did you have?"

Air hisses from the blood pressure cuff.

"I think she's throwing out her lunches," Adriana says. "Doesn't like counting in front of her friends, but she won't tell me. I pack a healthy lunch."

Adriana's right about tossing out the lunch, but poison is hardly healthy.

"How old is she?"

I'm officially not in the conversation.

"Nearly sixteen. Sixteen this Friday."

"A Halloween baby." The doctor smiles at me, and I stare through her. "And has she ever been evaluated by a psychiatrist?"

"She's had appointments, but won't say anything to the doctors. If she does it's only to explain how it's my fault." Adriana rubs her hands over her eyes and sobs again.

The doctor's gaze drifts to my lips. Then she writes something on the chart. "I'm going to send you to psychiatry for an assessment, just to be sure we're not missing something," she says. "A nurse will come by when it's arranged and explain where to go."

"Are they going to keep her?" Adriana asks.

I glance up. *Keep me?*

"I don't know for sure but, yes, they'll probably admit her," the doctor replies.

I start counting as fast as I can, shaking my head. They can't just leave me in here. Not in the Dark Wood. How will I find my way? This is just what the wolf wants. What Adriana wants. I pound the pillow with my fist. I fumble for my phone, but the doctor disappears. Adriana's crying again, but now it sounds like with relief. She's the stepmother in Snow White, having ordered the huntsman to take me into the woods and return with only my liver and lungs. He didn't. No, he left me for the wolf.

I keep counting. Once started, I can't stop. Why didn't the doctor wait for me to finish?

The Goth boy stares at me, and I give him a what-are-you-looking-at stare right back.

"I'm dead," he says in a dull monotone.

"Pardon me?" Adriana asks, but he keeps staring at me.

"You're dead, too. Look at your veins. They're blue." He points at my forearms where dark veins run their lengths. "You're rotting like me."

I glance to Adriana, hands clasped and praying that she won't leave me here.

Adriana's stopped crying now and squints at the boy before standing to pull closed the curtain that rings my cot. "Crazy," she says with an uncertain smile. "You're not rotting."

. . . ninety-nine, one hundred. "No," I reply. "But I will if you leave me here."

Chapter 3

I cling to my stepmother's wrist, hating myself for having to use Adriana for support. Her gold watch digs into my palm.

When she pulls her hand away to push the intercom button and announce our arrival, I wobble in my Converse sneakers. She lowers her arm, and I clutch the wrist again. We stand in the cold, green hall. An emerald tunnel with everywhere for a wolf to hide.

"I can't help you anymore, Milly," she says for the billionth time, as if saying so makes it true. "It's just not safe . . . Isn't this a nice color? It would go well with your bedroom's red curtains. Green and red, they're complementary colors."

Blood on leaves. I quake. What threatens to take me to my knees now isn't lack of food, it's the sign. And the doorway. Hospitals are warrens of doors. It's taken half an hour of counting to reach this one. Each time with Adriana waiting, her eyes judging as I count.

Pediatric Psychiatry reads the sign. I know what that means. A ward for crazy kids. Not me, not Milly Malone.

"Here she comes, start counting please," Adriana orders.

Through the small, mesh-covered window in the door, a shadow approaches.

With a click, the door gapes toward us, traversing the shiny arc on the floor where it has passed many times. It squeals over the linoleum like a pig at the sight of food. The woman in the frame wears a hospital shirt printed with pumpkins and witches, a stethoscope, and black slacks concealing a pair of flats. With her hair in a severe bun, I already know what she's planning to be for Halloween.

"Romila?"

One, two, three . . .

"She prefers Milly," Adriana says and holds out manicured fingers that stick from a vascular hand attached to a birdlike, gold-watch-encircled wrist, connected to the arm of a total bitch.

"I'm Nurse Stenson."

Everyone stops and waits.

Thirty-three, thirty-four . . .

"You found us okay?" The nurse continues; clearly she's been briefed on my quirk.

This is how it normally goes. The patience only lasts for so long and, at some point during the first thirty to forty count, the conversation fillers begin. As if I'm not here, not counting. I know their talking invites the wolf. It's all I can do to hold it back.

Fifty-six, fifty-seven . . .

"Yes," Adriana replies with way too much emotion. "But the cost of parking is robbery."

"Don't we all know it. Funding cuts have hit hard and the hospital needs upgrades, built in the seventies."

Eighty-five . . .

"We're looking forward to having her." Stenson's words cover my whispering count.

"So am I," Adriana says. "This has been hard."

She's telling the truth. She really can't wait for the hospital to have me—the psych ward.

Then they pause again, as if I *must* be coming close by now. I know what Adriana's wondering . . . am I counting to speak, or counting to go through the door? Because you can't do both at the same time. Obviously.

. . . ninety-eight, ninety-nine, one hundred. "Call me Milly. I don't belong here. Adriana's the reason I'm here. You want to talk to her, go ahead. Being here will only make me worse. Adriana wants to dump me. She wants to be rid of me while my dad's overseas so she can stop feeling like a failure at motherhood. In my opinion, you can't fail at something you're not."

One, two, three . . . Counting also buys me time. Time to take in what's surrounding me. Time to gather my thoughts, which are a bit sluggish these days. With each count I surf a wave of anxiety.

The nurse smiles at Adriana, who doesn't say a word—swallows hard. At home, she'd be nagging at me for the next hundred count. Here, she's either so close to being free of me she doesn't care, or she's on her best behavior, trying to reassure Stenson that my presence on a psych ward has nothing to do with her.

Rather than say anything further, the nurse spreads her arms like bat wings and points down a hallway. Recessed lights glow like a soft moonlight haze.

I stare at the nurse as I count and wonder if she will hold my gaze. Adriana never does. Within the first thirty Adriana always rolls her eyes and then starts shuffling her feet. The nurse looks away too. I'm a bit disappointed. That was a test.

. . . ninety-nine, one hundred. I edge to the threshold, hold my breath, shut my eyes, and hop to the other side. A chill runs through me. Is my spell working or is the wolf letting me slide deeper into its lair? Biding its time. With my eyes open again, I search for places where the wolf could hide. A corridor to the left leads to two doors with tiny windows framed in them. They remind me of prison cells. Another door is to a washroom. The only escape is the door behind me.

"Acute patient rooms," the nurse says, pointing down the hall.

For the *really* crazy.

At the corner of the two hallways stands a thick, glass-armored nursing station. I bet an axe couldn't break it. Another nurse busies herself behind the barrier. It's so quiet. She's fiddling with charts, stickers, and markers. It could as easily be a kindergartner's craft project. The nurses are safe. They have their burrow to retreat to, but what about me?

Someone, something, howls, and it echoes down the hall from the acute rooms. I lean against the wall and draw deep breaths. Adriana gives a hesitant smile.

The patient rooms are labeled with nurse names. Room 3A, Nurse Stenson. Room 3B, Nurse Abby. Eight beds total, four per room, plus the acute beds. One psychiatrist, two nurses, eight patients. And I wonder about the number eight. There were probably eight beds in the ER too. Eight.

"Hiya!" A black girl bounces in front of me, having come out from a toilet stall that's still flushing. I'm sure she's a patient, but the *Tina* engraved on her hospital nametag suggests otherwise.

"Call me Tink! Do you like ping-pong?" She flits from foot to foot. As her hands hold mine they're clammy with cold water. I'm surprised that she's touched me, but touching isn't a big deal so long as I'm not counting at the time.

One, two . . .

"Tink is our Recreation Therapist," Nurse Stenson says. "Tink, this is Milly. For today, we'll let Milly take some time to familiarize herself with the ward and meet with Doctor Balder."

Ward—there's that word again. Eighteen, nineteen . . . Once I've started counting, I can't stop. If I do, the wolf will have its chance. And it will swallow me. Sometimes I feel like a bomb with a looping timer. I can never be defused.

We continue along the hall; the nurse points out the showers. I catch a trace of mold and force away the memory of the gym change room. "The doors to the bedrooms don't lock, nor those of the washrooms or showers," Stenson explains. "Be sure to mark them 'In Use.'"

Adriana pales. "Is this a coed ward?"

"Yes, but we can't have locked doors," the nurse replies as if we should understand the reasons for this.

. . . one hundred. "The ER doctor said I was here for an *assessment*," I say. "Not necessarily to stay."

"The doctor will be a few minutes," Nurse Stenson says. "In the meantime I thought a tour might be in order, but you should know that an assessment can require a stay, too."

I snuff Adriana's smug smile with a glare.

Beyond the washroom and shower are two interview rooms, windowless with the exception of the ones inset into the doors. More cells.

My foot crunches over shards of a broken mirror. Stenson frowns, peering through the interview room window. As we pass, I spot a small, shattered frame in the far corner of the room, mounted to the ceiling. A talon of mirror reflects back at me. Someone is in for seven years of bad luck.

"One of the kids here," Stenson says. "He's harmless, but he really doesn't like those mirrors. They're not supposed to be breakable." Even Adriana's brow furrows at this. Nurse Stenson retreats to the nursing station and I hear her request a cleanup.

Thirty-three . . . A boy, easily two hundred pounds, almost six feet tall and wearing a pink tutu over his sweatpants, sways down the hall. I rub my eyes.

"Fairy, fairy, witchy-mirror, tralalalala!" he sings in a falsetto. He's pretty much the saddest fairy I've ever seen. With one leg in a plaster cast, clearly his mirror-bashing bad luck has already begun. His tongue protrudes from his mouth a little as he skips past, half on his toes, half thumping on his cast.

Fifty-two . . .

"Hello, Peter." The nurse smiles as she returns. "This is Milly. Please use your crutches." He pirouettes into 3B, ping-ponging off the doorframe without stopping. As the door shuts, I see that it's thick—almost bank-safe thick.

Seventy-seven . . .

"This is the cafeteria," the nurse says. It's just a room with some tables and a hole in the wall through which the food is probably served. The hole would make a cozy hollow for a wolf to skulk. It's on the ward somewhere. I can feel it. "If Milly stays, she will have a sitter. The doctor will go over the eating protocol." Adriana seems to know what this means, but I don't and no one is explaining it to me. "And here is the recreation room."

I squint into the room and ignore the other kids. The lights above have the buzz of night insects. The dark green walls are like a glade in twilight. Two boulder-like couches dwell near smaller armchairs. Cords trail from a television to charging game controllers. A ping-pong table and shelves of books, crafts materials, and board games overgrow the room. The two windows don't open, but the view looks out over a forest. The Dark Wood. So close. In a tree, crows. Eight of them. Eight again. What was that poem? It's in my book of tales.

One for sorrow, two for joy, three for a girl, four for a boy, five for silver, six for gold, seven for a secret never to be told. Eight? *Eight for I can tell you no more.* For secrets. What for a hundred? A hundred crows, that would be a murder for sure.

A few kids stare at me from where they sit in a circle in front of a woman with a red streak in her hair and a clipboard on her lap. When I take in the kid with no hair and the one dressed like he's headed out to a nightclub, I've seen enough and shrink behind Adriana.

"The rec room's where we conduct most of our group therapy sessions," Stenson says.

"Very nice. You'll make friends here, Milly." Adriana beams. As if she'd love to have this crowd over for dinner.

"Would you like to wait here, Milly? While Adriana signs some forms?" Stenson asks.

Forms? My heart picks up speed. Galloping now. There's no chance I'm only here to talk to the doctor. I know what I need to do.

. . . ninety-nine, one hundred. I hear the click of the outer door unlocking at the far end of the hall. But I've been counting to speak and can't use it for the door. Adriana's arms fold across her chest as she waits for my answer.

"No ping-pong, no Peter, no this," I say, pointing at the group. "No, no. I'm not some dancing fairy, bald kid. And I sure as hell won't be friends with any of them."

Another howl from deep in the ward sends a shudder through me. My wolf hunts.

The kids smile, their eyes alternating between wisdom, amusement, and boredom. The youngest looks my age. The eldest, with the headed-to-the-nightclub hairspray disaster and shimmering tight clothes, has a patchy beard; he grins at me while chewing gum and says, "She's right. You people are all dumbasses. Let's blow this pop stand, Chiquita banana."

And then I'm sprinting, and I have more energy than I thought, because I run into all two hundred pounds of Peter with enough force that he stumbles back. I roll around him and dodge the nurse emerging from the station. She's holding a broom and dustpan.

Thirty-five . . . This is as fast as I can count and still keep the wolf back. The outer doors have opened on some mechanism and once started they don't stop either, just like me. Inexorable. A juggernaut. I'm going to make it. I brake at the door and hear the swish of the nurse's slacks rubbing together.

Sixty-two . . . I think Nurse Stenson already knows how

19

much time she has. "You don't really want to leave, Milly. Not until you're better."

And I hear her: if I were better, I'd be out of here. I'd be on my way, hitchhiking across the country, crazy Chiquita banana on the lam. Counting towns, not time. I want to leave, but stepping through now means stepping into the Dark Wood.

In my stomach, a knot tightens. It's tied with my emotions. When the knot twists, my lungs hitch and I gasp; the sluice of my tears opens and drains, and the pegs in my knees are pulled out so that I struggle to remain upright. The nurse's hand lands on my shoulder. It's a caress. A manacle. I jump, cry out, and miscount.

I start over . . . cold fingers clutch my intestines and pull. "No," I say. My count's so weak. The spell is nearly broken. I sob.

"Do you want to sign the papers, Milly?" the nurse asks. "It would be a good first step."

I shake my head as fat tears roll down my cheeks. The door's still open, but I'm anchored to my hundred count.

"Family time is from four to eight," Stenson says to Adriana, who signs carefully without reading the forms.

"Visiting might be a bit awkward due to late meetings," Adriana says. "But I'll do my best."

The exit door shuts.

I'm trapped. I finish my hundred and have nowhere to go and nothing to say. So I scream.

Chapter 4

I'm in an acute room. That means I'm really crazy.

At least I'm safe here. I sit on the bed with my knees to my chest and lean against a cool cinder-block wall. I'm waiting for Doctor Balder.

The small window in the door looks out at another wall and the bathroom I share with the second acute room. There are no other windows. A light caged against the ceiling shines on me. Furnishings include a sink, a desk, a chair, a bed. That's it. The chair is molded into the desk and the desk screwed to the floor. A kid could go insane in here. *I'm hilarious.* I'm relieved. No more doors to pass. No one to talk to. I've calmed. I've dried my tears. They offered a sedative, *how nice of them*, but I passed—I need to be alert. I think Adriana eyed it longingly.

My stepmother isn't here. She's set up a laptop in an interview room to get some work done. I really can't believe her. She couldn't give a crap about Doctor Balder—maybe my screaming fit convinced her to stay, but more likely she only wants to be on record as having been motherly.

Oh, Mark, your daughter is in such good care, she'll say. *The doctor said she'd be better lickity-split, it's all in Milly's head. Nothing some pills can't fix. Wasn't your ex depressed, too? These things run in families.* She says passive-aggressive stuff like this all the time.

I hate her. I hate her talking about me with my dad. I want to talk to him, and pull my phone from my pocket to text him. I don't have to count before I type or tap—*that* would be crazy.

"Milly."

I jerk back. It's Stenson again.

"Sorry, but I need your belt. No belts. No shoelaces. And your phone."

I swing my legs off the bed. I hesitate handing it all over. Anything that can be used as a weapon against the wolf.

. . . "I need to text my dad," I say.

"You can call him on the unit's phone."

I think Stenson likes that I don't talk much. The belt whips out of its loops. I press an old model iPhone into her palm. I grip the device for a moment longer before relinquishing it. When you need to count to a hundred to speak, losing the ability to text is like losing your voice. My relationship with Bill is half hearts and emojis.

"We want to help you, so you don't need to text," Stenson says as she holds up the phone. I stare, and she turns to avoid seeing that I'm counting as fast as I can and want to respond. She doesn't get it. She can't help me. It's been three years. "The doctor will be here in a minute," she says as she leaves. It's not fair. I haven't had another turn to speak and slap my palms against the wall in frustration. But Stenson's gone.

I've seen enough doctors to know that a *minute* can mean a

lot of things, so I'm surprised when the door opens a moment later. "You the new patient?" The man at the doorframe wears a long white coat, jeans, and yellow Crocs. "I'm Doctor Balder." Doctor Balder has just showered, his cheeks are ruddy as if from a recent shave, and he's familiar. I've seen him, but I can't place from where.

One, two, three, four . . .

"It's wonderful to have you here," he says with a bright smile missing one tooth. "I see you're whispering, are you counting? Is that it?"

He sits on the edge of my bed, close to me, within inches of my thigh and leans in to listen to my count. It's nice not to have Adriana here, but it's also weird. I'd figured it was a rule or something.

"What brings you?" he asks.

Doesn't anyone pass information along in a hospital? I roll my eyes but keep counting.

This guy doesn't have my chart and looks like a junior resident, not even close to being out of medical school; come to think of it, he doesn't even look out of high school, but he's from India or something and they age well. His knee bounces like a jackhammer.

My lips are flying . . . ninety-eight, ninety-nine, one hundred. "I fainted during gym class. My stepmother brought me here, because she's totally out of her depth and thinks I have every possible eating disorder, and I'm probably psychotic too, because I have thoughts about wolves. So, let's just say I'm here against my will, because my dad has to travel for work and leaves me with that witch."

The doctor laughs.

I blink with surprise. I've never had a doctor laugh at something I've said.

"Evil stepmother, eh?" He laughs again. "Witches and wolves. Wow, sounds like I need to prescribe you a bow and arrows. Is there something you want me to do while you count? Count along, maybe?"

This doctor's crazy—maybe it runs with the specialty—but he's the first person who has ever asked me what to do while I count. He doesn't wait for an answer and starts counting aloud. I make it to a hundred before he even reaches forty.

. . . "Maybe you can juggle? I never see the w—"

"A hundred already?" he asks.

My fist slams down on to the bed. I start to count.

"Oh, I can't interrupt. Sorry, won't happen again, but while you're counting, let me add a few more questions, I do have other patients to doctor and all. Very important person. VIP, I am." He checks over his shoulder to the door as if the patients might be watching. "When did you start getting your period? What size bra do you wear? Have you lost your virginity? Please remove your T-shirt for the mandatory breast exam."

I really wish I could count faster.

"Vanet? Vanet!" Another man in a white lab coat enters.

Doctor Balder jumps up off the bed and holds up his hands. "I've got this one, doc," he says. "Anxiety disorder. I'd prescribe her twenty-five milligrams of Zoloft. Nurses just got some free samples in of—"

"Vanet, go back to your room and I'll talk to you later."

My jaw hits the floor. The guy named Vanet—or is it Doctor

Balder?—turns back to me. "Just wait, you'll see I'm right. They'll throw some drugs at you and observe what happens. First they clean out your mind with drugs and then they'll fill it with their own thoughts."

The other man takes Vanet by the shoulders and steers him toward the door. An impish smile spreads on Vanet's face and, as Adriana steps to the doorway, he whips off his lab coat. She cries out as the half-naked boy writhes, running his hands over his body and fluttering his tongue at her. "Vanet," Doctor Balder says, and then Nurse Stenson pushes past, grabs Vanet by the wrist and drags him out of the room. "Thank you," the doctor calls after the nurse. Turning back, he gives a big smile.

What big teeth you have, Doctor.

"*I'm* Doctor Balder," he says. "That was another patient and I'm very sorry."

I feel a little like vomiting.

"What just happened?" Adriana demands.

Balder sits in the chair, leans over to tuck a corner of the sheet back into my mattress, and then smiles again. His teeth are big and blocky. Adriana probably likes the edge of silver at his temples, setting off a neatly coiffed black mane. His skin is dusky brown, eyes even darker. On his coat are painted small silver stars. "I *am* sorry," Doctor Balder says.

"This is unacceptable," Adriana replies.

The doctor's lips pinch together, suggesting he'd like to move past this. Adriana folds her arms across her chest. He says, "Great. Welcome. Nurse Stenson tells me you've had the tour?"

I nod, still reeling from Vanet's total invasion of my life. I even told him about the wolf. I recognize him now. He was part

25

of the group discussion and, seeing fresh meat, must have rushed to shave and shower to disguise himself. Another wolf in sheep's clothing. If my head weren't quite so fuzzy, I probably would have figured it out sooner.

"Milly, can you tell me about what happened at school?" the doctor asks.

I lower my gaze and stare at the tiles.

"She collapsed," Adriana answers for me. That's fine. I've resolved not to talk while she's here.

"Had she hit her head? Did she lose consciousness?"

"The class was preparing to play some ball game. Milly slumped to the floor as she entered the gym. The school called the ambulance and I met her here, that's all I know."

"So she might have hit her head?" He starts peering at my scalp and picking at it as if searching for fleas.

"No, you can see she's underweight—she has an eating disorder." *I don't have an eating disorder.* Adriana flinches from my I-hate-you stare. "I just can't help her anymore. She makes me count with her for everything. Doors, to speak, every bite she eats. Her grades have really slipped and she's lost most of her friends."

"Milly, do you need to count before eating?" he asks. "Do you feel you have to?"

I stare at his shiny black shoes.

"She says that if she doesn't, bad things will happen. Terrible things. It's a *feeling.*"

Balder makes a series of notes and nods. "And is there anything else she wants you to do other than counting?"

"Mostly the counting, counting to take a bite, to chew, to

take another bite. Oh, and she has to see the ingredients laid out for the meal. I check everything ten times like she asks, but I just can't do it anymore. It's too much."

More notes. "Well, then I would like to keep Milly a little longer. To clarify the diagnosis, to get her weight up. Sometimes compulsions like counting can be eliminated simply by nourishing the brain." He taps his noggin. "Which doesn't perform well without energy. How does that sound?"

Adriana looks like she's won an award. That's it? Five minutes and the jury's back in? "Compulsions—you think she has OCD," Adriana says.

"Possibly Obsessive Compulsive Disorder, and if so, with a mild antidepressant and psychotherapy we can work toward reducing the frequency and severity of her OCD thoughts and related anxiety."

I begin to swing my head back and forth. I don't want to stay here. It's not my fault, it's hers. She can't handle it. She brought me here. To all the doors. I wouldn't have freaked out if there weren't so many doors. At home I'd be texting Bill—how is staying here going to help me meet new friends? Or help my grades?

"Can you come back tomorrow, Mrs. Malone?" Balder asks.

Mrs. Malone was my mother.

"Milly will need a few things," Adriana says. "Tomorrow after lunch."

I might as well not even be here. My insides frost. The wolf skulks nearby. I twist the bedsheet in my fingers. I feel the wolf. It's here. Nowhere is safe.

When I look back up, they've moved the conversation into the hall.

Chapter 5

Adriana disappears with a promise to return with a new toothbrush. Nurse Stenson brings me an assortment of books, but I don't feel like reading. I zone out a bit. Maybe I am rotting inside. If that's what it takes to turn the wolf away, maybe it's not a bad thing.

Lunch arrives with another patient apparently included in the menu. The nurse who was leading the group session enters my room, pushing a gurney carrying a comatose blonde girl. With the food wedged near the legs of the girl, it's like she's part of my meal. All delicate and pale fleshed, a dessert rather than an appetizer, but still tasty for a dragon. The nurse is more of a main course, plump and roast brown.

Between the nurse's wide bottom and the extra bed, she struggles to bring in an IV stand trailing behind them. Her shirt is swarming with black cats flashing hundreds of little claws and teeth.

The nurse smiles. "Lunchtime. I'm Nurse Abby. Sorry, space will be a bit tight, but we can't spare two sitters." I have no idea what she's talking about. "Why don't you try a bite," she says, pointing at the girl—or the food, I'm not sure.

Nurse Abby slides the tray onto the desk, draws in a deep breath and shimmies on her tippy-toes to the end of the patient bed where she sets to connecting an IV line with a port in the girl's wrist. Everyone's eating. From beneath tinfoil the food smells of butter, chocolate, and gravy.

Feeling a little like Hansel being fattened for the witch's ovens, I slip into the cold chair and start counting. The nurse sits and smiles at me while I whisper to the food. . . . "I want to make a phone call," I say when I'm done.

"Okay, after your dinner I'll set you up with the unit's phone," Nurse Abby replies.

The wolf would like nothing more than for me to be like the girl on my right. Poisoned and helpless. Counting cleans the food of the insidious shadows. It is part spell, part antidote. It keeps the light on. I remove the foil and steam billows from peas, thick gravy-covered meat, and mashed potatoes so buttery they're golden. In the corner, a dollop of whipped cream tops pudding.

I take a small bite of potato and count to a hundred as I chew. Whenever I finish a count, the wolf veers away, only to creep back. I ask, "What's wrong with her?"

Nurse Abby smiles sweetly, but shakes her head. "I'm sorry, we can't talk about the conditions of other patients."

A half hour later the IV bag's empty and the nurse clears my tray, stacking it on top of the patient before pushing her out. I ate a few bites of each item—a balanced meal. "Back in a minute for that phone call," she says.

She returns with a can of Ensure, a meal replacement, and

sets it on the desk. The message is clear. Finish the can, make your call.

Despite the chalky flavor, I can drink much faster, and ten minutes later she waits at the door for me to leave.

"All calls are taken outside the nursing station," she says. "We don't listen."

Sure you don't.

Under Nurse Abby's dark, watchful eyes I hop into the hallway.

"Wait at the corner of the station, and I'll hand you the phone," the nurse explains.

I try to keep to the wall so that no one from down the other hall can see me. It's mostly quiet. A door opens and closes, but it's not one of the bedrooms; I can see those doors. I sense that I'm being hunted again and wonder who is in the second acute room. The one who howled.

"Dial nine out," the nurse says.

I jump, but she's holding the phone through an opening in the plate-glass window.

Snatching the phone, I count to a hundred, and then dial my dad's hotel in Japan and ask for his room. It's morning there.

"Mark Malone," he answers. Leaning against the wall, I knock the receiver three times so he knows it's me.

"Milly? Hurry, honey, I have to leave soon. I hear you're having a rough time."

. . . "Dad—Dad?" I keep my voice low and hushed. "Adriana's imprisoned me on a psych ward. It's not okay. You have to get me out of here. I'd be fine, if I were home and didn't—"

"Milly, I know," he interrupts. My knuckles whiten against the receiver. "I've spoken with Adriana and I want you to give this a try. She's bent over backward to try to help you."

One, two, three . . . Adriana told him. Liar. She didn't wait for me to talk to my dad first.

She's poisoned my own father against me. I start to cry, and I can't count and cry. But I've already started counting so my stomach roils at the thought of miscounting, and I struggle to concentrate on that rather than listening to what my father's saying. Nurse Stenson walks past with a straight face that says she's trying her best to give me some degree of privacy.

Fifty-six . . . I catch the odd word he's saying. *Business. Work. Home soon. Help. Trial. Counting. Unhealthy.*

A door clicks. It's behind me, where Stenson went. Out of the door of the second acute room emerges a kid in a wheelchair. He wears a turban and, for a boy of no more than eighteen, he has a significant beard. His eyes are dead though. Cold splotches. I shudder and look away as he's wheeled past.

. . . "Get me out of here, Dad. Please." A tear dribbles down my cheek. "You should see these people."

"I'm sorry, Milly, I have to trust Adriana. I'm sorry, but I must go now."

This is how every fairy tale starts. With the storyteller explaining to the reader just how it is. *There once was a girl named Milly who was the wolf's coveted meal. Whose father left her in the clutches of an evil stepmother. Whose stepmother imprisoned her with monsters.*

My dad doesn't wait for me to count to say goodbye. I've never felt farther away. The phone bleats.

"Are you done, dear?" Nurse Abby asks and I nod. I can't call Bill, not like this.

I've been trying to decide what to tell him. I mean, who wants to admit that they're on a psych ward? *I blacked out for a week. I have no recollection of anything. But my belly button's a little sore and I wonder if I was probed . . .* That won't do, not alien abduction. *I awakened to a giant fairy hovering over me, his name was Peter. He explained that he'd lost his wings and asked if I would quest with him. The poor fairy blubbered so terribly that I agreed, and soon we set off and found a little cottage in the woods where a young woman slept and would not wake. Sound familiar, Bill?*

It's important that I find the right story, because who the heck wants a crazy girlfriend? He's been good to me. Understanding, while I count. Without him I'd never be invited anywhere.

Before I turn away, I sense someone watching—not the wolf, someone else. I risk a step beyond the nursing station and see the Goth boy from the ER, watching me from the end of the hall.

Rottengoth. His cloak of darkness is gone, but he's sheathed in black. And he stares.

I slink back to my room and read for a few minutes. The nurse enters with a toothbrush and toothpaste and a message from Adriana that she'll come back tomorrow with my bag. I don't care that she doesn't give me the toiletries herself. Before squeezing the toothpaste, I inspect the security seal. Satisfied that it hasn't been tampered with, I brush my teeth and then read until my eyes close. Reading helps me to fall asleep, but the wolf shatters it, filling the night with terrors.

The sleek-furred wolf's limbs can disjoint, allowing it to slip anywhere. And the dreams are always wherever I am. They follow me. Are dreams not meant to help the dreamer? Then why must mine consist of such torture? Tonight's nightmare starts with me peering through the window into the second acute room and the hairy-faced boy lurching into view, his smile wild through the glass.

Then the wolf's chewing his neck. Behind them flits a shadow. I squint, but miss it. I can't tear myself from the boy's blank, sightless eyes.

Chapter 6

I wake gritty-eyed with Nurse Stenson taking my pulse. She makes a mark on my chart.

"Good morning." Doctor Balder looms in the door, stars on his coat and his smile overwhelming the yellow light above the bed.

He takes the chart from the nurse. "Romila, how was your night?"

One, two, three . . .

"She had some bad dreams," Stenson says.

The nurses are always watching. Stenson the witch and Nurse Abby, her feline familiar.

. . . "I want to leave. Just let me leave. I'm being punished for nothing. Nothing I did. I'm not hurting anyone. This is Adriana's fault."

Balder taps the chart before speaking. "If Adriana's the cause of your problems, then staying on the unit will make you feel better. If things continue as they are, you risk losing your friends, failing school, and maybe even death. We can help you here."

Death? Did he say death? . . . "But, don't you see? I don't have a problem. When I'm home, I'm fine."

At home I'm like a blind person who knows where the furniture is. At home the wolf can huff and puff all he wants, but the house is made of brick reinforced with the mortar of my counts. Despite Adriana's invasion of our family, it's still my mother's home. My mother's couch, drapes, table, cushions sewn by her hand. It's where she died and her must permeates the air.

Stenson and Balder share a look and then the nurse leaves. Balder settles in, taking a seat on my bed. "Will you try something for me?" He doesn't wait for an answer, just plows on. "I want you to think back a few years." I nod. "Did you play any sports? How many friends did you have? Did you have any hobbies or were you a part of any clubs at school?"

He means three years ago, before my mom died. I'm not stupid.

. . . "I remember playing soccer and basketball, but everyone went competitive and I wasn't that into it. I had more friends, sure, but they all became stuck up and started caring about shopping and makeup, and I'm more into things like music. As for hobbies and clubs, I read. I still read. There was a debating team, but that grew sort of geeky."

I redden at the memories.

"Okay, you were more actively involved, had more friends, and none of your compulsions were interfering back then."

. . . "Yeah, but they don't stop me now either."

He grunts like I'm not saying what he wants me to. "I can appreciate that you'd rather not be here." His eyes widen and hands reach out, palms up in understanding. "I get it. No one likes to be sick. From what we know, you're not eating enough because you require a hundred seconds to take a bite, another hundred to chew, and another hundred before you can take another bite again."

I shake my head, and realize I've forgotten to start counting and begin. I can't remember the last time I did that.

He keeps talking. "A hundred seconds to speak, and a hundred to pass through a doorway with a few other rituals." He holds up his hand. "Don't worry, today isn't about figuring out why or changing anything—or throwing drugs at you. Today and tomorrow are just about getting to know you and helping to find ways that can make this stay here as easy on you as possible. Do you think you can do that?"

. . . "It's a hundred *count*, not a hundred seconds, that's a big difference. And as for these *rituals*—your word—lots of people need to do things before they eat. Half the world prays before they can eat, don't you know?"

But Balder's moving on. "Perhaps you can walk me through the morning you fainted, what happened, step by step."

. . . "It was gym class."

"And do you like gym?"

. . . "No, not really."

"You seem fit and you used to play soccer and basketball, why don't you like gym?"

. . . "Well, I have to pass through a whole bunch of doors to get in there, not to mention the change rooms. I'm always late, so the teacher makes me do push-ups. Then there are the lines on the floor, I guess I try to avoid them too, and there are lots of lines."

He writes that down. "What happens when you're faced with lines and doors?"

. . . "I . . . I get this feeling . . . like everything is about to rip in half, if I don't count. Like it's all up to me to stop the big bad wolf from clawing the door off the world."

"Did you feel this way before you fainted?" I give him a thumbs-up. "How do you feel now that you've had some nourishment? Better?"

. . . "Yes, all better, now I'd like to go home."

"If I were to ask you to walk through this door, how would you rate that same feeling, compared to the one on the day you fainted being a ten?"

. . . "An eight, but with the door I'll just count and the feeling goes away."

"And without counting?"

I shudder.

"Okay, Milly, I do think you can leave the acute room and join the other patients."

A flush of dread pours through me. An eight. Eight crows for *I can tell you no more.*

"Your fainting yesterday likely was due in part to lack of food and dehydration. We're going to work on this first." The whole time he's speaking he's looking me over, like his eyes are feeling me up. When my leg twitches, he glances toward the motion and makes a mark on his page. What if he's a pedophile? Would you go into children's psychiatry, if you were? You betcha. "You'll have someone sit with you at a few more meals, just to ensure that you're eating. He'll stay with you for half an hour after and you won't be able to use the washroom for an hour, so be sure to go before your meal."

. . . "This sitter thing is creepy. I'm not anorexic. Just slow.

37

Are *you* crazy? A man watching me while I eat is *not* going to speed me up. It's—"

"Romila—" It's my stepmother at the door.

First rule: Don't interrupt me.

I growl a little and start again. One, two, three . . .

The doctor checks his chart. "Good morning, Mrs. Malone?"

Dark smudges shadow Adriana's eyes like she was partying all night. She seems smaller somehow, even though she's trying to appear indignant. "I thought the next meeting was this afternoon." Her hands clutch her hips.

"I'm sorry, I always start privately with the person who will be staying and then speak to the family," the doctor says.

Her lips thin. "Romila's only fifteen, an adult should be present."

"At this stage, we're going over notes from the ER doctor and nurses, clarifying, explaining how meals will be served. Making sure she's taking in enough food is our first order of business. We'll help Milly settle in and then try to figure out what's making her life a struggle, before trying new interventions to see if we can help Milly build a more liveable life for herself."

"She skips meals at school. It seems pretty obvious what's wrong. She's anorexic and she's losing weight like crazy."

He begins to write and I'm shaking my head, counting madly. See, Adriana likes to control the message. Go off message and she grows angry.

Adriana's flying along. "At home she uses her counting to get out of everything. Meals, chores, homework, talking to me. But it's out of control now, that's why we're here. But you have more doors than rooms in this hospital and with so many people, I can't see how she'll improve until you start actually doing something to help her. What am I supposed to tell her father?"

"We're here to help *Milly* become healthy," Doctor Balder replies.

I hear the emphasis on Milly and I'm sure she does too.

"I just want my life back! I want her to be normal," she says.

Normal.

I'm done my count, but I'm speechless. This is the real Adriana, and I'm glad the doctor was here to recognize it.

"I'm sorry," Adriana says. "I've tried everything."

Adriana breaks down and disappears somewhere to compose herself. To my surprise the doctor doesn't follow after her and remains focused on me. From the chart he pulls a sheet of paper with two columns and lays it flat on my desk.

"Okay, Milly, what I'd like you to do for me is to map out every time you feel the need to count, hop, shut your eyes, anything that would be out of the ordinary for, say, one of your friends. Next to that, write a number. That number will be a rating of how anxious you feel."

How close the wolf is . . . .

"Do you think you can do that?"

I nod.

"Good, that's your homework. You can meet your bunkmates after lunch."

Adriana doesn't return, but a short man with no neck and bulbous eyes appears, carrying a tray of eggs smothered in cheese with another can of Ensure that says it's chocolate flavored, but I know isn't.

"Sitter," he says.

Todd is written on his nametag. Without another word, he sits on my bed and points to my food. I hesitate, and he points at my fork.

When I finish counting and only take a nibble of egg, he harrumphs. I don't like having him here and will slow-eat in protest. I work on my crazy-map between bites.

When do I feel anxious? When do I need to count? Crossing doorways, before I take each bite, to chew, before I speak or dial lock combos, when I open a book, or dial a number—these are all doors of a sort. As for ratings, they're pretty much sixes and sevens, except real doorways. Those are eights.

It's not much. Not really. I have to hop through while I close my eyes and hold my breath, but who doesn't lift their feet and hold their breath while passing a graveyard? How else are you supposed to keep the evil spirits from possessing you?

After an hour of watching me touch cheese to my tongue, Todd leaves with my tray. I smile after him. Milly: 1. Todd: 0.

It's too late to call Bill, but what would I say anyway? I spend the rest of the morning reading. When I stop, I remember where I am and can't believe I've fallen so far. I'm on a psych ward. Anger at Adriana builds and then burns off just as quickly. I can never hold on to rage long. The ward is the worst place for me. It can't make me better, but somehow I feel as though I shouldn't be surprised it's come to this.

Nurse Stenson takes me to my new cell.

Chapter 7

3A.

The room's empty with the exception of the comatose blonde I met earlier with Nurse Abby. Everyone else is in some sort of group therapy about managing anger. The blonde's still sleeping and, from the look of her, she's been here a while. Over her bed hang get-well-soon cards chock-full of angel wings and crosses. The cards are an anomaly; every other wall is entirely blank—the same forest green of the halls. An empty IV bag droops on a rack near her bed. The sheets on my cot are so taut I need to use all my weight to untuck them. Adriana would be impressed. My bed's beside the sleeping girl's, pushed up against the windows. I can hear the sleeper's breathing—long, quiet breaths.

This room has windows that look out over the park, the Dark Wood. They don't open. I assume it's so that no one can throw themselves out.

Four beds. One occupied. I wonder who my other two bunkmates are. Two tables with four chairs and four chests of drawers are all the furnishings that can be crammed in here. One table has English work spread out, and I realize that they still want us to be doing homework. This is like the most awful, boring camp ever. I bump into a chair. It doesn't move, nailed to the floor. So is the table. I'm so screwed.

I sit at the homework table. The chair is just far enough away that I can't sit comfortably while I read over the top pages. The essay is on fairy tales as a way of communicating fear. Wolf as the devil. Wolf as the pedophile. Wolf as the stranger. The work is a loose scrawl full of grammatical errors and half thoughts. I can't stop myself from slipping commas and semicolons into a dozen places. It passes the time. When I'm done, I fidget and pick at the skin on my arms until they redden.

On the table opposite me lie a few doodled-on pages, but no work. Ink drawings of the skeleton of a house, what looks like a graffiti tag, which could read RED, but it's hard to decipher, and a loping wolf that starts out small at the tail but expands until half the page is its jaws. I swallow at that. I can hear it growling, and the more afraid I grow, the louder it growls. I shudder, rubbing at the gooseflesh on my arms. My mother had lots of stories with wolves. Now I remember the stories better than I remember her.

She told me one about a country devastated by a terrible wolf. *One day, the king proclaimed that whoever killed the wolf would have his daughter's hand in marriage. Two brothers accepted the king's challenge and entered the forest from opposite sides. When the younger brother came upon the wolf, he slew it with an arrow shot and placed the wolf around his shoulders to show the king. As he left the forest, he came upon his elder brother, who had given up his hunt. Seeing the success of his brother, the elder waved the younger over and begged him to share a skin of wine. They drank late into the night until they both lay down to sleep.*

At the midnight hour, the elder brother crept from his bedroll and slit his brother's throat. He buried him near a stream where the earth was easy and then took the wolf to the king, who fulfilled the promise of his daughter's hand.

Years later, the course of the river changed and the waters uncovered the bones of the younger brother, which were come upon by a shepherd. The shepherd took the bones to the magistrate, who had the power to speak with the dead. Soon the identity of the killer was known. The king executed the eldest brother and hung his skeleton for all to see beside the wolf's pelt.

How handy would it be to be able to speak to the dead? I think the skeleton was supposed to be a reminder. That the truth always comes out. *Does it, though?* Everyone here sees me as the problem. No one sees the truth. The whole thing reminds me of what Vanet said about prescribing me a bow and arrows.

Not being particularly artistic, I leave the drawings alone and keep snooping through the room. I run the tips of my fingers across the tops of the drawers but don't open any. The sleeper's breathing hitches, and I shuffle over to investigate.

The breathing is so shallow her chest barely rises and falls. Soft breath tickles my palm as I hold it over her mouth. Unbidden, an image flashes into my mind of my hand pressed down hard on her mouth, fingers pinching her nostrils. I count to a hundred to banish the thought. I'm so messed up. I wonder if she'd wake.

Everyone pictures this. Stabbing your mom as you hold the knife. Throwing your brother over the edge of the cliff, picturing him cartwheeling on the way down. Or stepping off after him.

43

Twisting the steering wheel so that the car slams into the concrete barrier. We all have urges. Right? I'd wondered the same thing, thinking about holding a pillow over my mother's face as she lay dying. When she wouldn't *just go*. Guilt flushes through me, hot and nauseating. Bile burns in my throat.

Someone's at the door. I snatch my hand away and sit back on my bed. At first I think it's a boy because she's bald and squarish shaped, but I'd pretty much look like a boy if I had no hair too. He's a she. Tattoos of flame tongues twist up from her chubby wrists, disappear under a really old T-shirt with more holes than fabric, and then lick out of her collar.

The girl walks in wearing jean shorts, her thick legs sporting way more hair than her head. Her nose, brow, lip, and ears have enough hardware to set airport security on edge. As she enters, I see that the stains on her pants and shirt aren't stains. The edges of the holes are blackened, and I smell a touch of char on her. She looks me up and down and says, "I hear you're the new nut. Welcome to the nut club."

I count as I observe her.

"You may be mute, but it doesn't mean it's okay to stare—I might snap." She jerks forward, making me flinch. Already it's unclear how much she's benefiting from the group therapy session on controlling anger.

"I'm Pig," she says.

I'm not surprised by the nickname. She's porky, short, and bald, but not on-chemo-bald; she has a thin fuzz of hair all over her scalp. Her nose isn't piggish, but she watches me with hungry, beady eyes that remind me of a pig's.

"No staring, remember," she says, and when my gaze swings

away from her to the comatose patient, she adds, "Sleeping Beauty. She doesn't do nothing. Just takes drugs. We decorate her sometimes."

"I watched Stenson stick a needle in her neck."

I turn at the new voice. The girl at the door is drenched in crimson clothing. Dark bruises have settled into the wells of her eyes and a stitched cut on her forehead has scabbed over. "The syringe didn't have anything in it. The nurse did it just to see if she'd wake up."

"Liar," Pig says. "This here's Red."

Red's shoulders are up near her ears as if she's trying to fold in on herself, but she twitches every so often and her head pokes out higher and her back straightens. Even though I'm sitting, I can see she's way taller than me. The twitching reminds me of a pump-action shotgun. Her stringy, brown hair is shaved on one side and drapes down the other side of her face.

"Want to try poking her?" Red nods over at the sleeper, whose thin lips have puckered upward as if she waits for a kiss. Red's dresser and desk have a settled-in appearance with photos, the nubs of pencils, and bits of eraser dotting the surfaces.

I'm halfway to a hundred.

"Check out her lips," Red says, squinting at mine.

"She retarded or something?" Pig asks.

"Skinny, real skinny, I'm guessing anorexic."

"Score," Pig says. "Finally I might get a decent meal."

It's like they're skinning me. . . . "I'm Milly. I'm not a retard. I have to count to a hundred before I can say anything, or walk through a doorway, or eat. So I usually say a lot all at once and then shut up for a while. I don't want to be here and think I'm going to try to escape. My stepmother dropped me here and my dad's traveling, so I'm not sure where I'll go. Why do you have no hair? What are you all in for?"

"What did she say her name was?" Pig asks.

One, two, three . . .

"Oh, I get how this works." Red's voice is flat and emotionless.

"How what works?" Pig's eyes lock on mine.

"She's counting. Like she's stuck," Red explains.

"That's stupid. Can she still hear us? GO TO YOUR REAL MOM, IF YOU HATE YOUR STEPMOM SO MUCH," Pig shouts.

Red shrugs. "I don't want to talk about any crap anymore, who cares, she might not be here long enough to make all of this waiting pay off. I'm so tired of this sharing shit anyway."

Pig cracks her neck, still looking at me. "I burn it," she says. "My hair. So they cut it short. I like to burn stuff. I got until the weekend here and then—" She smacks her palms together and then makes as though her hand is taking off, all without breaking our stare. "Burning rubber."

Burning, I realize, finally catching on. Pig's here because she burns things. And *she's* about to get out.

I finish my count. "I'm Milly. My mom's dead," I say. "Died a few years ago."

"You were right, Red," Pig replies. "I'm not sure the waiting is worth it."

She sits down at her table and evidently decides to give me another shot. "I'm a prisoner," she adds. "It's this or juvie. But once I'm outta here, I'm the daughter to the McDonald's family.

Richie, rich, rich. If you're all nice to me in here, I'll make sure you're cool once I'm out. Free milkshakes and nuggets for my *hos*."

She's lying. What's not obvious is what she's hiding.

"Christ, you both need help." Red buries her head beneath her pillow and pretends she's asleep.

"Thoughtful of them to put an Ana in with me," Pig says. "My complaints about the lack of food have borne fruit. Or at least extra French fries and chewy Jell-O. On the escape front, good luck buttercup."

The smell of cigarette smoke wafts through the doorway and triggers the patter of footsteps.

Pig runs back to the door and draws deep breaths.

"It's a conspiracy of the gum companies!" a voice calls out. It's Vanet—the fake doctor. "The gum companies paid for all those studies against nicotine and they injected people with cancer cells when they were sleeping. You're all part of it. Do you own gum stock? Do you?"

Pig looks back. "He's so crazy. Craziest. After you, I'm thinking. But so hot. I don't smoke. But I love the smell of it. If you smoke, bum them from Vanet there, his brother sneaks them in."

I catch the grin on her face as she peers down the hallway as if hoping to catch a glimpse of Vanet.

. . . one hundred. "Don't think I can escape, Pig? I almost did yesterday morning. You're a pyromaniac, aren't you? You're here because you burn everything." I lift my hands to the ceiling. *And that makes me so not the craziest person here.*

Pig shakes her head. "Way to go, Sherlock. You're pathetic.

Close to escaping? I saw. Too bad you freeze every ten seconds." She steps close to me and whispers in my ear. "The only thing that escapes is Wolfgang from his acute room, slips like smoke through the crack under the door."

From beneath her pillow Red growls. My eyes fly wide, and I nearly trip on my count. *Wolfgang?*

"Wolfgang doesn't try to really escape the ward though, it's just to get to us. Or you." Pig snaps her jaw open and shut.

My hundred count is up and terror flows thick in my mind. Wolfgang's room is only forty feet down the hall. Did Vanet tell them about my wolf after our little interview? My eyes narrow.

. . . "No wolf's going to eat me in favor of you, Pig. Even I get a little hungry looking at your thighs."

Pig swings her butt around as if she'll sit on me, and then bursts out laughing. She laughs until tears stream down her face. "Yeah, I guess you're right," she says. "One day I'll be caught in a fire and roasted, and everyone'll want a piece of me. You're all right . . . What do we call you?"

She waits me out, never breaking eye contact.

. . . "Milly, I said already. Milly."

Chapter 8

"Feedback group!" Tink bounces at the door. "You don't have to come, Milly, but you can if you want. No pressure!"

From beneath her pillow, Red groans and then throws it off. "Actually I do have something to say. Why is it that I have to go when Sleeping Beauty over there can fake sleep and get away with—"

"At group!" Tink springs away. Following her is Peter, who flaps his arms like wings and drags his broken leg behind him across the floor.

Pig points at him. "He's here because he's suicidal. Believes he can fly like a fairy, so he jumped from a third-floor balcony."

. . . "He's not suicidal then, he doesn't want to die, he wants to fly," I say and both of them stare at me. "What's feedback group?"

"So you can like pre-count, if you know you're going to say something?" Pig asks.

I nod my head.

"Oh, but *now* we gotta wait again. How are you even alive?" Red says and walks out of the room, adding, "Come see for yourself what this is all about."

When I stand up, something beeps. Pig has started the timer on her watch and follows behind me. I turn to stare at her as I count. She stares back. Beady eyes unblinking.

When I'm done I say, "Please don't." And start counting again.

Pig huffs and walks out.

A minute later I shut my eyes and hop across the threshold of my room. I really miss my phone. At school I usually don't have to talk; I text instead.

Tink's high-pitched voice squeaks about how everyone's opinion is highly valued. I use the washroom; that's four doors to pass. Even washroom stall doors count. Even cupboard doors count, but not drawers. Drawers are different. No hinges.

After I jump into the rec room, everyone goes silent. I'd love to be rid of the jump; it attracts so much attention. The TV's on, and Peter is too close to the screen to see anything more than a blur. Rottengoth stares at me with his mouth open. Pig's watch beeps; she timed me anyway.

Vanet laughs. "What ho? She has to hop, too? That's pretty sexy, isn't it, heh? Like a Playboy bunny hops, and we gotta hop back to what we were talking about, right? Hop to it, Tink. Time is money."

Tink presses her hands to her forehead. "Welcome, Milly. Who would like to explain for Milly's benefit the purpose of feedback group?"

Everyone stares at stained ceiling tiles or interesting spiders climbing cracked walls, so Tink says, "This group's a chance for everyone to contribute. Here you can put forward requests and opinions about the unit, and please no comments on other people's thoughts."

I nod because I think she expects me to, and then she taps her pencil on her clipboard.

"Okay, everyone, so we have one request for marijuana on the ward from Vanet."

"Medical marijuana," Vanet says. "Big difference, they've done studies and it's actually good for you. Cures cancer. Do you think Milly would hop if she was hopped up on it? Or Red have her nightmares? Pig would probably burn even more stuff." He mimics lighting a joint and then talks on. "But I wouldn't be as busy, know what I mean, Tink? No fairies smoke up, so Peter over there would crash and burn. Totally do not, I say, do not, give any to Sleeping Beauty—she's so relaxed already, she'd probably break into pieces. Contraindicated."

"Thank you, Vanet." He looks as though he is about to speak again, but Tink holds up a hand. "A request for more fairy movies from Peter."

Pig snorts. "Yeah, more home movies for Peter. That's what we need."

"Red wants Theresa to join us even though she doesn't respond, and Pig wants us to have parties and no singing of Disney songs allowed in common rooms, ever."

"I am just saying we should celebrate more. You know like birthdays, and Hanukkah." Pig adds, "Without singing."

"Hanukkah? I'm not Jewish," Vanet says.

"Your name's Vanet," Pig replies.

"That's not Jewish," Vanet says. "I'm black. How can a black kid be Jewish? Jewish people are from Israel and they don't have a single black person there. Not one."

I hear a siren and, if we weren't already in a hospital, I would have assumed they were coming for nearly everyone in this room.

"If *you're* black, then brown is the new black," Red says.

"When you first came in, you said you were God. Is God black?" Pig asks.

Peter starts laughing in the corner.

"What's funny? So what if He is?" Vanet says, leaning forward in challenge.

"Do you still think you're God?" Red asks.

"I don't think I'm God, but one day I'll be president," Vanet replies with a hand to the ceiling as if he's won the election already.

"Is that close?" Red asks.

"Heck no. But close as we can get," Vanet replies.

"There is no God," Rottengoth says.

"God," Pig replies, pointing at Rottengoth. "For sure. Wesley's going to Hell."

"Can't be worse than this," Rottengoth says.

Tink sits there, blinking. "Thank you," she says. "Just a reminder that this is feedback group. Wesley? Feedback?" Rottengoth's eyes flick to Tink and his tongue scrolls around the inside of his cheek.

"Well then, a good session." Tink claps her hands. "Anyone for ping-pong before dinner?"

Good session? I have no idea what even happened.

Jumping up, Tink races to the ping-pong table as if to reach it first, but everyone drifts away from their chairs, some shouldering past me, others slumping on the couch and ignoring Peter's protests that his fairies are disappearing from the screen.

Only Rottengoth remains. He's thin and Asian-looking. His straight black hair hangs past his chin. On him, the cut's girlish.

Everyone here seems a bit jumbled in their genders, as if nature didn't quite decide and we'd prefer to be something society says we're not. Or maybe we're all a bit of everything—didn't I once wish I was a fairy? A knight?

Rottengoth stands, walks over to me, and stares into my face. "Sixty-nine, eighty-five, twenty-two, one, two, three, eighty-eight." Then he walks away.

Looks as though Vanet has already told the boys about my counting too. I hope he's going to Hell. Still, Rottengoth seems better than the last time I saw him.

I sit down on the couch in front of the television.

"Aren't you supposed to be running from wolves?" Vanet asks. He's playing an Xbox game that involves collecting gems and jumping around. "I'm the best at this," he says as he shoves the controller this way and that as if the full body movements help. "I could be the top player in the world, if I bothered. Thousands of fans. Sponsorship. Ferrari tried already."

His character dies. "You're distracting me. It's hard to play with a girl coming on to me the whole time."

. . . "Vanet, you're a jerk for pretending to be my doctor and worse for breaking pretend patient-doctor confidentiality and . . . and if you were the last computer game champion on earth, I wouldn't be interested."

"Sure you would," he says. "I'm learning how to juggle like you asked."

I'm counting, and he lifts his eyebrows knowingly. Silence is acceptance, so I accept everything. I go for my phone so I can type out for Vanet the true depths of my hatred, but then remember it's gone.

I push off the couch and wander to the ping-pong table; Tink looks up hopefully, and then I curve away to the shelves. Everything from philosophy to comic books lines the wall unit. I pick out a Batman comic and start counting. I sit in a big corduroy chair and sigh, sinking into it, glad to lose myself in the exploits of the Joker or Catwoman.

"Milly," Stenson says. "Your mom's here."

I clench my eyes.

"Her mom's dead," Red says from another chair.

"Thank you, Red," Stenson says seriously. "I made a mistake. Milly, your stepmother is waiting in your room."

I don't want to see Adriana, but Vanet now has his shirt off and is doing push-ups. No—he's dry humping the floor with Pig watching. I try to block the visual with my hand as I make a beeline for the door.

Two hundred counts later, Adriana unpacks a suitcase into the chest of drawers beside my bed. Despite each garment being crisply folded in the suitcase, she shakes them out and refolds them, forming sharp creases that always take forever to fall out whenever I wear them. There's neat and then there's crazy neat. Maybe Adriana should check herself into the ward.

"I brought enough for a week," she says. "Sorry about this morning. I had to leave."

The clothes she's obsessively folding were my favorites a couple of years ago, when I refused to give them up even though they are too small and worn out. I bought them with my dad, when Adriana and my dad first began dating. In the beginning, their relationship had been okay; it was as though I'd gained a big sister, but then she became my stepmother and I realized how

54

much I missed my real mom.

Nothing she's unpacked is dance-worthy and at the end of the week there's the school dance.

"The dance," I say. "I want to go to the dance. And I don't fit into those. I'll need a costume."

She holds up a blouse and a skirt. "But . . . these are your fav . . . well, they'll have to do for now. And if the doctor thinks you're ready for the dance, then you can go to the dance."

If my dad were here, I wouldn't have to ask her; he wouldn't care if I went to the dance.

Her narrow face regards me tiredly. My dad picked her because she looks like my mom: blue eyed, brown, straight shiny hair, with the same bangs my mom had before hers fell out. But Adriana's younger and, although my mom was never really fun, Adriana's even less so.

"I brought your book of fairy tales." She places a thick book with a frayed spine and gold lettering on the dresser top. I step forward and take the book, holding it to my chest. My mom and I read it together at bedtimes. Before she really faded at the end, she told me that everything I needed in life could be found in fairy tales. Its pages are smooth like vellum and smell of ancient power.

. . . "I'll be out in less than a week," I say.

"Of course you will." She puts a new bottle of shampoo and conditioner on the dresser. Enough for a month. "In a week you won't have to count anymore. And you can walk right out that door."

It sounds like a curse. Or perhaps an impossible task like in the fairy tales. *To succeed, Milly, you must fight the wolf neither clothed nor naked, neither riding nor walking, neither in night nor day.*

So I'll be seeing the wolf somewhere around twilight, while wearing a fishing net and with one foot on a bike, the other on the ground. That'll be some costume.

Chapter 9

"Dibs on sitting beside you at dinner," Pig says to me and then lingers at her side of the desk. While we wait for the meal to start, she fiddles with papers. My sense is that she's buying time to stay close to me. I rearrange everything Adriana put away in drawers, shaking out the tight folds and dumping the clothes back. Red tries to sleep.

"Wait a minute," Pig mumbles. "Who did my homework?"

. . . "Helped," I say eventually.

"I love you," she says, smiling beneath her pinched eyes. "You're going to feed me and do my homework? Today keeps getting better."

"Dinner," Todd says at the door. He's wearing jeans and a blue collared shirt, except you can barely see the collar due to the shortness of his neck.

"It's Toadie," Pig announces.

Toadie has a wide gut and head. Big, fat lips squat beneath a flat nose. He pauses in the doorway and his distantly spaced eyes blink at Pig.

"The sitter," Pig finishes. "What's for dinner, Toadie?"

"My name's Todd," he says in a nasal tone. "Milly and I are acquainted."

Pig is already on her way to the door. "Acquainted? Big word for a sitter. I still can't believe people get paid for this. Did you grow up thinking, 'You know what I wanna do? I wanna sit and watch people not eat?'"

"You just lost your off-ward privileges, Eleanor."

"Never had any. Call me Pig." Her eyes light like coals.

"Call me Todd," Toadie challenges, but seems to shrink at the same time.

"I'm sick, I'll burn this place down if you don't call me Pig. You'll lose your job. I'll tell them about your slimy fingers always touching me."

"No one believes you anymore," Toadie says.

"Maybe not, but every report needs to be investigated, doesn't it, Toadie? What *are* you hiding?" Toadie's lower lip protrudes as he considers this. "That's better." Pig winks back at me.

. . . "I'd be careful, Pig, you know the story about the chicken?" I ask.

"Yeah, the one that wanted to cross the road."

. . . "No, the fairy tale—" I say and I'm about to continue when Pig cuts in.

"There's no chicken in fairy tales. Lots of pigs and wolves, a few frogs, but no chicken."

. . . "There is in mine," I say and throw my hands up to say "forget about it."

"So why do I care about a stupid chicken?" Pig asks.

I ignore her.

"Let's have it, tell us about the chicken fairy who showers us with McNuggets with the flick of her wand," Red says.

. . . "It's not a chicken fairy . . . never mind. It's about a man who doesn't want to share his roast chicken with a friend and so hides it when he comes by. After his friend leaves, the man takes it back out again, but it's turned into a toad that jumps on his head. The man is forced to feed the toad every day or else it will eat his face."

Sometimes I feel that my wolf is like the toad. I have to keep feeding it my count or it'll eat me, eat everything.

"That's stupid," Pig says. "Toads have no teeth."

"Watch out, Pig, or I'll eat your face." Toadie shows his chops.

"I'm telling the nurse you asked me to sit on your face," Pig says, and Toadie's eyes bulge even more. "Milly and Red heard you say it."

An orderly shakes his head as he enters and helps Sleeping Beauty into a wheelchair and places a bib around her neck.

I am counting and, by the time Beauty is in the hall, I'm ready to follow. The cafeteria door's another matter.

"Let's go, Count," Toadie says and smirks.

"I'm the one who comes up with names around here, Toadie. Leave Milly alone," Pig shouts from the cafeteria, without taking her eyes off the food other kids already have on their trays. She's waiting in line while a server slops dinner with a spoon.

I'm really not sure I want Pig as my protector. Does that make her my prison wife? One of the troubles with my counting quirk is that people miss the typical social cues they use to determine if I like them or not.

Peter stands with his tray in the middle of the room, his pink tutu flaring.

"Hey, Tweedle Dee, you want that dessert?" Pig asks, reaching for it, but she backs away when Peter lifts a fist.

I grab a tray and wander to the food. From a bowl of fruit that I don't need to wait in line for, I take an apple. When I move to turn away, Toadie says, "Tsk, tsk, a balanced meal, Milly."

"Yeah, Milly, for once I agree with Toadie. You have your friends to consider, too," Pig says. "It's all you can eat and no one charges for what you can't finish. Load up that tray."

A woman in a hairnet and wearing a black apron stands opposite the line. As we near, she warily looks us up and down like we might have discovered something sharp on the ward. Bins of food before her hold mashed potatoes, Salisbury steak, and peas. She spoons them into the divisions of my tray.

"Isn't this what we had yesterday?" Pig asks.

"Different gravy," the woman says.

Unlike Pig, I don't care what's for dinner or if the hospital food is good or bad. So much of our lives are food. Buying, growing, preparing, cleaning, cooking, spicing, eating, cleaning, making money for it. It seems ridiculous that we can't go more than a few hours without another entire meal of it. We're the weakest species. If everyone ate as little as I did, no one would go hungry.

My platter is filled with food. I think this is an important moment with Toadie here. He sits me away from the other two tables full of kids and folds his arms across his chest. This is a rematch, but with spectators. I have to show I won't be controlled in this way. If I can outwait Adriana, I can outwait anyone.

One, two, three . . .

"Would you look at her . . ." Vanet says. "She's casting a spell on us."

"She's counting," Pig says. "I'd starve."

"Oh yeah, counting to eat," Vanet says.

"It's weird," Red replies. "What happens if you don't count, Milly? Kaboom!?"

I try to ignore the banter. And Adriana wonders why I throw away my school lunches? How can anyone eat like this?

I lean my teeth against the apple and sheer a piece of skin, which I then chew.

"One, two, three, four, five . . . she counts a hundred chews, too?" Vanet asks. "Let me try that." He takes a big bite of steak and smacks his lips as he chomps. "Nom-nom-nom-nom." He lasts maybe fifty before he spits it out. "The only thing worse than hospital food is turning it into tasteless paste. Yuck!"

Luckily I don't hold Vanet's interest for long. Soon he and Rottengoth—who stared at his meal the whole time without eating—have left. My food cools, and gravy scabs over on the steak. Red complains of a headache and goes to bed early. Pig grows so frustrated that she stomps out, empty-handed, muttering about waste. Then I'm alone with Toadie. I haven't said a word. Not for an hour. Toadie's stomach growls. Ten minutes later, he gives in.

Toadie says, "They'll put you on an IV and then a feeding tube, you don't want that."

I've googled these things. I'm not there yet. But he's right; I don't want a feeding tube.

"You're going to miss evening group," he says, but I know I

don't have to go if I don't want to. A small part of me wants to. This place is like a terrible car crash you can't look away from.

I glance up, and he smiles as if he's found the lever he needs.

"Don't want to miss group, do you? Get to talk about your stuff and everyone else's stuff."

Nurse Stenson waves at us from the doorway. "Todd, group is starting. Dinnertime is over."

I pick up the apple and place it to my lips. Todd's eyes light in triumph, and he turns to hold up a hand to stall the nurse.

Toadie thinks he's won. But he hasn't. He reminded me that group means I need to talk. The only thing I want to do less than eating is to talk about not eating. Now it's a question of how slowly I can eat between now and the end of group. I bet half an apple.

Every time Toadie begins to shake, I rest my teeth on the skin of the fruit and draw them down until they harvest another thin bite. Vanet's right. Chewing a hundred times does suck the flavor from it. I swallow goo.

After a quarter of an apple, the nurse drags me into the rec room. More for Toadie's sake than mine, as his shift appears to be over. Two doorways, another five minutes. I count down slowly. And ask to go to the washroom even though I know the rule about no washroom for an hour after dinner.

By the time I enter, Vanet's really going strong, lips smacking as he chomps the nicotine gum. I'm surprised to see Red slumped in a chair, holding her head.

Tink interrupts Vanet as I enter. "Welcome! Sit, Milly. We're discussing favorite foods."

I turn back for the door, but Stenson steers me to a chair.

"Everyone has a favorite food," Tink says. "We're going around clockwise. Vanet, continue."

"I was just saying . . . imagine you're a pig and your favorite food is pork," Vanet replies. "You could eat yourself. Maybe my favorite food is human and I don't even know it." His gaze comes to rest on Pig.

"Don't even think about it," Pig replies.

"Wesley?" Tink asks.

Rottengoth sighs. Darkness still hangs from him, but more like a tattered cloak than a funereal shroud. "Apples."

"That's not real dark and moody," Pig says.

Rottengoth looks at me. He, too, understands that apples can be poisoned.

"Babies," Vanet replies. "Now that's gothic."

After Wes, it's me. My stomach clenches as I count. I feel as though I can't breathe deeply enough. . . . "Pizza," I manage to gasp out, and everyone turns. I surprise even myself. "My favorite food is pizza with pineapple and chicken on top."

"Chicken?" Pig shakes her head. "So our new friend here is richie, rich, rich. Not ham—chicken!" This from a girl who tells people she's a member of the McDonald's family. I'm not rich. Not poor, but not rich either.

Tink lit up, however, and she ignores Pig. "How do you eat it? Is there a special way?"

She wants to know if I have a weird ritual for pizza. I do. Everyone waits in silence except Rottengoth, who starts humming the Jeopardy waiting song.

"What are we doing?" Red asks when I'm halfway finished my count. "I mean, I'm not waiting for her to speak. Life's too short."

"How else is she gonna talk?" Pig replies.

"That's not my problem. She doesn't have to count, and she's not the boss of everyone."

"Okay," Tink says. "Why don't we create a rule for when we'll wait for Milly."

. . . , ninety-nine, one hundred. "Hello, you asked me a question, you have to wait. It's not fair—"

"You're not the boss of us," Red says.

I flush at the interruption.

"See, you cut in, and she has to start again," Pig says. "If we cut her off, we have to wait because that's already a group rule, not to interrupt."

Tink's nodding. "Okay, so if we address her directly, or if she is interrupted mid-thought, we'll all wait for her to count. Let's wait. Milly, how do you feel about that? And then let's move on with how you eat pizza."

"Yeah, I'm riveted," Red says, and then adds to Tink's raised eyebrow, "What? That wasn't sarcasm."

Vanet's rubbing his crotch.

. . . "Fine, whatever you want," I say. "As for pizza, first I have to line it up so that the point is square with my chest. Then I count to a hundred. If I stumble or skip a number, I have to start again. Then I take a bite, chew a hundred times, then swallow and wait another hundred before I can take a second bite. On pineapple bites, I count to one hundred twice."

"What if you don't count to a hundred?" Pig asks. "You explode or something?"

All eyes burn into me and my chest tightens. I don't even like talking about what would happen. That makes it more real. *What happens?*

"The wolf comes, isn't that right, Milly?" Vanet asks.

I shake my head.

Tink asks, "Does anyone else have a little ritual when they eat?"

"I'm guessing Sleeping Beauty prays," Pig says.

"Or maybe her ritual is having a feeding tube shoved into her stomach," Red replies.

They move on, going around talking about their stupid favorite foods, even though the whole discussion was really only for me. No one is waiting to hear what I have to say anyway.

Chapter 10

Before lights out, I read from my book of tales and feel stronger. I fall asleep listening to Pig's snores. Every half an hour or so, Red calls out, shouting words I can't understand. I don't hold it against Red; my dreams have always been vivid too. I toss and turn, and finally slide out of bed and into the cold hall.

I grip my book at my hip as the wolf slips a paw beneath the acute room door. Claws imbedded in callused lumps of black, brown, and gray fur scratch beneath the doorframe, gouging the linoleum, leaving curls of it behind. I have to count before I can even scream.

An entire leg flails under the door now, and I have no doubt that the animal can somehow fit its whole body through the thin crack at the door's base. As if freed by my thought—my acknowledgement that such a thing is possible—the forelimb disjoints with a snapping of bones and tendons and a mass of fur worms beneath to pulse in the hall. Like a battery of fireworks, the rib cage billows out, legs clack straight, a head snaps up, and the teeth of the grotesque, hanging jaw clap home.

"Wolfgang?" I ask it. "Are . . . did you—?"

The lift of its black lip silences me.

I open my book to page one hundred and start counting. The wolf growls. Yellow eyes stare at me without blinking and give the green corridor a fixed-from-under stare. I force myself to move and race backward to the nursing station, where the night nurse flips through a magazine between rounds. My count isn't working. I scream at the nurse, but she ignores my waving arms. When I turn back, I have reinforcements.

"Mom?" I scream and stumble from her.

She's putrid. Flesh hangs from her bones. Her fingers grip a barbed vine that cuts into the wolf's throat as it lunges. She hauls back, keeping me safe. But her eyes blister with cool disappointment. The vine snaps, and my mother leaps but only catches a fist of tail fur. The wolf lopes at me, head low between rolling shoulders. I drop the book and count to flee.

Backpedaling, I slap up against the door to my room. The wolf snarls as it passes the nurse, but she turns another page, unaware of the creature or the cursing reanimated corpse on the ground. The bedroom door slides open. I finish my count. I climb into bed and pull the blanket over my head. The cover rasps over my skin, rough from the heavy detergents used to clean it. Through a hole in the blanket, I watch the door reopen.

The wolf pushes into the room; drool hangs from slavering jaws and the snout sniffs the air. Then it snuffles Red's sheets, and she lashes out in her sleep. The wolf dances away from Red, over to Sleeping Beauty. It tests fangs across her neck, but doesn't bite down, only hooks canines on the slow pump of her veins. I wonder if it can sense whatever's wrong with her. Whether she's inedible. Rotting. Pig's bed is empty.

I'm the only one left. Where's my mother?

The wolf swings to me. It tenses, crouches, and springs. A roar tears from its throat as it pounces. I haven't counted; I cannot cry. Red screams. And I'm wrestling with my blanket, but nothing's there except a nurse shushing me.

"You've had a bad dream," she says.

I glance around. Light spills through the open doorway. My book digs into my side. The wolf's gone, except I know that it's not. Not really.

"Do you want me to stay? Get you a drink of water?" the nurse asks. I shake my head. "Okay, honey, take some deep breaths. Everything's going to be okay."

I don't want to fall back to sleep again, but I suppose I do, because I don't remember the nurse leaving.

The next morning, Nurse Stenson takes my heart rate and blood pressure.

"Vitals," Stenson says as the air hisses out of the blood pressure cuff. "Then washroom and breakfast. After that you'll have group, school—once your coursework arrives—free time, lunch, school again, after which visitors are allowed, dinner and group before evening free time."

. . . "When do I see the doctor again?" I ask.

"A nurse will come and get you." She moves to check Sleeping Beauty's vitals.

On my way to breakfast I shimmy over to the edge of the nursing station and peer down the hall to the acute rooms, hoping to inspect the floor for scratches. I jump back when the door opens. I hear squeaking and peek. An orderly is pushing the unshaven patient Pig called Wolfgang. With the orderly present,

I feel as though we're on sacred ground. I'm on the safe path. Wolfgang's shaggy cheeks are brown flecked with red, and the haunted stare sees nothing. Despite my dream, my counting spells must still be working. Perhaps it's my mother, still here, still holding things together. As the doors to the outside world buzz open for them, I shudder and hurry my count to enter the cafeteria.

In the dining area, I collect all the food on offer. When I sit, I pick up the banana. Toadie's face lights when I peel it in five seconds flat, but his delight sours as I stare at the fruit for a hundred count and take a tiny nibble from the top.

"You're kidding, right?" he says and I know it's a rhetorical question, but I answer anyway after a hundred to chew and a hundred to speak.

. . . "No."

Two bites later his face is in his hands. Toadie's vacillating expressions are beginning to make me wonder if they count as interruptions.

He shakes his head, but after another half an hour of nibbles, I think I've broken him. What's weird though is his eyes are bulgier this morning. It's as if he's grown even more toady overnight.

Finally, Stenson strides over when Toadie appears close to tears and places another can of Ensure on the table.

She snaps the tab on top of the can. "One every meal," she says and pushes the can to me. "Plus whatever you can manage during regular mealtime. If the can isn't empty, you'll be back to eating alone to reduce distractions."

I count under her and Toadie's supervision and down a good

third of the can in a single go. I don't want to eat in the acute room alone with the sitter. I don't want to eat anywhere near Wolfgang. Satisfied, Stenson walks away.

Vanet asks for a tea but doesn't drink any. Instead he snaps the string from the tea bag and begins to floss with it. "What?" he says when he catches my stare. "They won't let us have dental floss. And the water's never hot enough for tea anyway."

With my platter cleared, Stenson returns. "Milly, I'd like to introduce you to the thought board now that you're done." Stenson drags me back toward the recreation room. Once inside, she waves her hand at a large whiteboard. Tink's doing yoga with Peter and Vanet, who scooted ahead of me while I counted. Vanet's following Tink's sun salutation into a downward dog, but Peter seems to prefer the happy baby pose. I hate yoga.

"You can leave any thought here you want," Stenson says, holding up a marker. "It can be about your experience on the ward, or something you're having trouble with that day. Anything and everything as long as it follows the rules of the feedback group: no hate, no comments on the comments of others." She frowns before erasing a thought written in tight capitals. *How many patients have had sex with the staff?* I've been here a little less than forty-eight hours and I can already identify Vanet's contributions.

"Is there anything you'd like to write?" Stenson asks. "I understand that you don't need to count before you write."

I take up the marker and write: *When can I leave?*

Which she promptly erases. "It's not for questions about your treatment."

Someone else has written: *What happens to me if Milly stops counting?*

When I reach to smudge it out, Stenson stops me.

"It's a fair question," she says and so I write something I need to know.

Who is in the other acute room? I write. *What's wrong with him?*

Stenson smiles. "Sometimes people just need some quiet. You can go back there too, if the beds are not already in use. Just ask."

I shake my head.

"Okay, Milly, group in fifteen, why don't you wait in here so you're not late."

I hear Red in the hall, complaining about her headache again. She wants to skip group.

"Breathe in the good Karma and breathe out the liver toxins," Tink says as she lifts her hands to the ceiling. "Feel the poisons flow out of your toes and gather the sun's energy with your hands." The fluorescent ceiling light flickers. *Liver toxins?* This is why I hate yoga.

"I saved you a spot," Vanet says after Stenson's gone. "All kinds of good Karma right there." A mat lies flat in front of him. He's as far to the back as he can get.

. . . "There's no way I'd risk letting you stare at my butt," I say.

"What? What are you talking about? You think I want to . . . shocking!"

I don't look at him or bother responding. After a minute Vanet rolls up his mat and disappears. Tink, seeing her only true participant leave, smiles at me and then packs it in. Peter sighs on the ground.

With Stenson out of sight, I write in weird letters that shouldn't be traceable back to me: *Have you seen the wolf?*

And then I hustle away from the board. Peter's now watching from the couch.

"I'm a fairy," he says. His lips are thick all the way around, and his forehead slopes backward more than it should.

. . . "No you're not," I reply and then glance down at his cast. So what if he wants to be a fairy? Maybe he wouldn't have tried to prove it, if people had only accepted that he was a fairy.

"I don't like you," he says.

. . . "Okay, you're a fairy," I say and it's weird because it's almost like his brain needs a hundred count to process his response. For once, I can keep up with someone else.

"How do you know?" he asks, and I catch the plaintive note in his tone, as if he's begun to doubt himself. I wonder if he thinks he's a Disney fairy or a Grimm fairy. There's a big difference.

. . . "Well, some fairies like bread and butter. Do you?" I say, racking my brain for everything I know about them from the book of tales.

He nods tentatively.

. . . "And they don't like iron. Do you wear anything iron? Maybe a sword?"

He shakes his head.

. . . "There you go," I say. "And you know how sometimes people ignore you?" The smile that has begun to expand on his face drops. "That's because they can't see you. Not everyone can see fairies."

The grin returns. "I like you."

I smile back at him. Stenson starts pulling chairs into a circle, spoiling our fractured rhythm. She's hauled Red into the room with her.

. . . "You coming?" I ask Peter, and his eyes widen in fear. "Come on, it'll be fun."

"Peter can stay on the couch if he's more comfortable there," Nurse Stenson says without even looking over.

Peter's face dips.

. . . "You sure?" I whisper to him, and he gives the tiniest of nods.

Vanet walks in, smiling like he knows something I don't. He takes a chair in the middle, and Red sits on the edge of hers, nearest to the door. I didn't even notice Rottengoth sitting in the corner of the room reading, but now he stands and sighs into a seat. When everyone's sitting, Stenson folds her hands on her clipboard.

"Vanet, would you explain the rules of group for everyone?"

Red groans. "Really? Every time."

"Yes," Stenson says. "Every time, so don't be moaning every time."

"The first rule of group is . . ." Vanet drops to a secretive hush, ". . . that there are no rules."

"That must be a different group, Vanet. How about group therapy?" Stenson asks.

"Right, sorry." He winks at me. "That other one's clandestine. The first rule of group therapy is . . . don't tell anyone about group therapy. Contraindicated."

"Correct, in a way," Stenson says. "Everything said here is confidential and must stay within the group. Does anyone else have a rule?"

There's silence. I'm new so I'm not even counting to speak, but clearly no one else is going to help Nurse Stenson voluntarily.

She turns to Rottengoth. "Wesley, is it okay to interrupt someone, or to tell someone that they're stupid?"

Rottengoth shakes his head and breathes noisily out his nostrils.

"No," she agrees. "Respect each other. This is an open group where you can say anything without judgement." Stenson stares at us each in turn until we nod. "Most of our meetings have themes—yesterday we discussed anger, and today we'll be talking about fear. What do you think fear is?"

"Fear is the mind-killer," Vanet says.

"I'm sensing a book reference," Stenson replies. "But what do you think that means, Vanet. What is a mind-killer?"

"That it takes over like a parasite that eats ants' brains and turns them into zombie ants, then bursts out of their skulls."

"So it can take over our thoughts," Stenson agrees. "And it can make us do things we wouldn't normally do, and it can spread. Very good." My mouth is open in amazement at how neatly she fit Vanet's crazy comment into what she wanted to hear. "Do you agree with Vanet, Red? Is this always true?"

Red's shaking a little and looking beyond Stenson. Through her, like Red's somewhere else, seeing something else.

"I don't agree. Fear can make sense," Pig says. "You know, if a guy points a gun at you, fear can help you to run. On the street, there's lots of crap you should fear. Why else do you think I've made myself look so pretty?"

"Yes, healthy fear," Stenson says. "It can give us energy to flee, or strength to do amazing things like lift cars." Red's head snaps up at the mention of cars.

"What other fears are healthy?" Stenson asks. There's silence.

"Is it important to have a healthy fear of other cars, so we don't crash into them?"

My mom used to do this to me. I recognize the cadence of Stenson's questioning. She's using the Socratic method. She's going to keep asking questions until she reaches whatever reaction she really wants. Socrates was the father of all trolls.

Red's feet jerk off the ground and slam back down. Her arms are folded across her chest and her eyes tight shut.

"Red?" Stenson probes.

Red's eyes open up, and she shakes her head at the nurse.

If last night's food discussion had been for my benefit, then I have the sense that today Nurse Stenson's trying to draw out Red.

Rottengoth starts blathering, "Crash, smash, fire, burn, choke, dead, rot, worms." He looks down at his hands as if they've already decomposed.

"When are fears unhealthy?" Stenson goes on and nods to me.

Pig answers. "When they stop you from doing the things you should," Pig says. "Like Milly and her counting. She can't do stuff quick, because she's scared."

I'm waving my hand around to get them to wait.

"Milly?" Nurse Stenson asks.

. . . "Listen," I say. "It's not like I can't do stuff. I know my counting seems weird and doesn't make sense to you, but it's not a *problem*. I can still move around and text people and play video games."

The kids don't look like they believe me.

"Thank you," Stenson says. "Compulsions are a little different from fears or phobias. Phobias are fears that started out as rational but have grown so that the amount of fear is far greater than the situation calls for. The phobia prevents us from doing things. Compulsions are things we feel forced to do even though they're due to an irrational fear."

"Don't be so *irrational*," Pig says to me and chuckles.

I'll take irrational over crazy any day.

"I'm scared of falling," Peter says from the couch.

"Yes, Peter, another fear that is based on rational fear," Stenson replies over her shoulder.

"Unless you're a fairy," Vanet objects. "Fairies shouldn't ever fear falling. Fear of falling for them doesn't makes sense—they can fly. It's irrational."

Stenson holds her breath as if trying to maintain patience.

"And wolves," Peter adds. "I'm scared of the wolf."

My head whips around, but Stenson just smiles and continues on, which makes me wonder whether she's avoiding the issue of the wolf on the ward or just anything Peter says.

"What makes you frightened, Red?" she asks.

Red swallows.

"I know," Vanet says, and before Stenson can stop him, he pulls out a toy car from his pocket and makes a sound like a bomb going off.

Red leaps up, snatches the car from him and hurls it across the room. Then she bursts into tears and sprints out the door.

"She's scared of dinky cars," Vanet says, nodding. "And for good reason: Thousands of people die every year choking on dinky cars."

Peter giggles. "Dinky."

Stenson's mouth thins to a slit. "I think that's enough for today."

Chapter 11

Vanet and I are the last to leave the circle of chairs. Group was weird, but I actually get what Stenson was going for, that fear can be good or it can take over, it can be the mind-killer. Maybe she was talking about me too, not only Red. But I don't run screaming to my room anytime someone brings stuff up.

"That was mean," I say to Vanet.

"You know what's really mean?" He pulls his sleeve up to his shoulder and flexes his bicep. Striated muscles cord and then smooth. "It's dancing around the real problem. Like Red, like you and your wolf. That's what you need to hunt down. People may call me manic because I don't think enough before I do or say stuff, but I know it's what everyone else wishes they could do." He points to his bicep.

"Nice," I say. "Listen, if I don't count, people will die."

"'Cause of the wolves. Last I heard wolves can be killed. You only need to give yourself the license—Wait!" He slaps me on the shoulder and races over to the craft table.

I roll my eyes. He's got markers out and a sheet of paper.

Tink is ushering everyone out to start schoolwork, but I don't have any yet, so she leaves me be.

"Vanet—now," she orders.

As he passes, he presses a folded paper into my hand. When everyone's gone I open it.

Hunting License

Milly is licensed to kill one wolf for forty-eight hours by any means necessary.

I press the sheet against my stomach, before refolding it and shoving it into my pocket. *By any means.* There's the problem. No one has prescribed me my bow and arrows.

I read while the others do math and English exercises. You could hear a paw step. Only the staff chats at the nursing station, and every once in a while that goes quiet and Stenson pokes her head into the rec room and smiles at me.

After lunch I try ping-pong with Peter. Peter's not very good. In the corner, Vanet throws tennis balls into the air. He can manage two, but whenever he adds a third ball, they all come tumbling down. A few minutes go by before Vanet comes over to watch us play. He sits on the arm of the couch. His eyes never leave me.

"It's not going to happen, Vanet," I say. "I'm so not interested in finding a boyfriend on a psych ward."

Rottengoth looks up from his book. "Shh."

But it's wishful thinking, because Pig joins us, wringing her hands and rubbing her bald head.

"This is more like it," Vanet says, looking around. "No Stenson."

Peter knocks a serve over, but to his great disappointment and my surprise, I slam it back.

"What's the worst thing that's ever happened to you?" Vanet asks everyone.

Rottengoth says, "Group's over. Leave us alone."

It's the most coherent thing I've heard from Rottengoth. The stack of pills I watched him take at breakfast must be doing something.

"Did I ask you?" Vanet replies. "You're not invited, you just happen to be here."

Peter knocks a second serve in and it's such a rare event that I let the ball zing past. He hoots.

"I'll tell you," Pig says. "You all know I'm rich and if I had my hair you'd probably even recognize my mother because she's pretty famous. She couldn't keep me. If she had, she'd have lost her modeling contract and her engagement to a prince. A Saudi prince. Wait . . . I guess that's the worst thing to happen to me, not being recognized as a bastard of the Saudi Kingdom. It's not what I was thinking, though. Someone stole my backpack while I was sleeping in a bus shelter once. That was bad. Everything gone."

Vanet whistles. "Lucky she dropped you off at the local McDonald's for adoption, heh?" Then he pokes me with a finger. "You counting? 'Cause I'll talk first, if you're still below fifty." I wave him on. "The worst for me was when I was boning this chick and she's like all screaming because it's so good—"

Pig's giggling and snorting.

"What?" he says. "I'm like huge."

"Prove it," Pig says, her eyes lingering below his stomach.

Vanet stands up and starts circling his hips in a striptease.

"Duh-nana-na-NA! Duh-nana-na-NA!" he sings.

Pig starts jiggling with laughter. I have my hands over my face, but I'm peeking through the fingers. A nurse checks on us just as Vanet's wrestling with the fly of his jeans.

"Vanet, keep it to yourself." It's Nurse Abby, the one with the red-hair streak. She's wearing a top covered with crows rather than cats today.

"We'll finish this later, Pig," Vanet continues. "Like I said, though, this chick, she's screaming and suddenly she goes rigid, completely like-a-boner-straight, she told me afterward that the orgasm had been so big that she'd had a seizure. But I didn't know that, I figured I'd pounded her so hard that my shlong had gone through her. Right along her spine and I had killed her with my massiveness." He stares back at me. "How about you? Anything that bad?"

I put the ping-pong paddle down and shake my head. . . . "My mom died."

"Yeah, I heard, but sometimes it's tough to know if you're better off or not. Maybe you'd just have two people disappointed in you like Wesley has," Vanet says.

Rottengoth lifts a fist and then pretends to crank his middle finger up. Vanet's an asshole. Suddenly the hunting license in my pocket doesn't feel like anything more than a sheet of paper.

"All right, next question for the group," Vanet says. "What's your dream?"

It's weird, because I feel lighter being allowed to think about an answer. Everyone seems to lean back and look to the ceiling. It reminds me that these people may all be crazy, but they're still people. With dreams and fears.

Pig's first to reply. "After I'm out of here, I'm going to start a chain of restaurants called Pig's. They're going to compete with my family's chain—McDonald's."

"My dream is to go to fairy world," Peter says. "I want to fly to fairy world. Everyone is happy."

"Yeah, that sounds nice, Peter," Vanet says. "Jump off another building and you may get there sooner rather than later."

If my counting were finished, I'd leap on him.

"That's a stupid thing to say, Vanet." Pig shakes her head at him and turns to Peter. "Don't worry, Peter, fairies have to master short jumps before they can do big ones. Vanet doesn't want you to see fairy land."

"Sure I do! It's his dream," Vanet says. "Who doesn't want to get their dreams? Think of me as your fairy godmother, offering sage advice and wish fulfilment."

Vanet's like some stoned fairy godmother who's as liable to kill you as help you.

"I don't have any dreams. There's nothing left to do," Rottengoth says, and it's as though his darkness shrouds him tighter again.

. . . "What do you mean?" I ask, having hit one hundred just as Rottengoth spoke.

"We're not at war. The mountains have all been climbed. There isn't anywhere that hasn't been mapped. Why bother doing anything again?" Rottengoth replies.

"You could do it better," Vanet says. "Well, try anyway."

He shrugs. "Better, faster, bigger, that's why we're in this mess."

"What mess is that?" Vanet asks, swinging an arm around the room as if it's the height of opulence. "This place is awesome."

"The world, doorknob. If everyone relaxed and didn't worry so much about the next iPhone, we'd stop making things no one needs."

. . . "I agree with Wes," I say, having counted fast. "Everything sucks. Climate change, terrorism, no jobs. I mean our parents really dealt us a crappy hand. And we can't do anything about it." *It's a Dark Wood.*

"You can find a cure for cancer," Pig adds.

"I suck at science. What's the chance I'll do anything useful for the planet?" Rottengoth replies.

I happen to agree with Rottengoth on that too, but stay silent. Bide my time.

"Well, you're not going to do anything, if you don't try," Vanet says.

If I don't go out into the Dark Wood, my life will never begin.

"What if I don't care to try . . ." Rottengoth says.

"I guess tough noogie," Peter says. And everyone looks to him and bursts out laughing. Peter gives a proud smile.

"How about you?" Vanet asks me.

Everything quiets as they wait.

. . . "I don't have dreams. I only have nightmares," I say.

It must have weirded everyone out, because they all sober.

"Buzzkill," Vanet says. "Save that for the Stenson group."

And I guess I am a buzzkill, because everyone leaves. I head for the bathroom. But when I finally open the door, there's Vanet on the toilet with his pants down, stall door wide. He's jerking off. He's forgotten to slide the sign to "In Use," or maybe this was what he wanted.

I can't even cry out. I slam the door shut. *Doesn't he ever stop?* I take the hunting license from my pocket and crumple it into a ball before tossing it in the garbage.

Chapter 12

While the other kids go back to homework, Nurse Abby ushers me into interview room one. Doctor Balder's there with his notepad and his wolfish teeth. He pushes a book my way, *The Rock-on Anxiety Workbook.* Great. I trade him my crazy-map, which he scans.

"This is good. This is very good. Take a chair, Milly. How's your first full day with the group going?"

. . . "I'm not sure I belong, Doctor Balder," I say. "I mean, there's nothing really wrong with me."

"I agree," he says and I look up in surprise. "Nothing's really wrong with you. Nothing so wrong that we can't help pretty quickly with the problems you do have. Once you come onside with a combination of drug treatment and behavioral therapy, we'll get you fixed up." His smile shows each of those giant teeth.

. . . "But that's just it. I don't need drugs, or therapy even. Fainting was annoying, but you have me drinking those meal replacements, and I promise to keep doing that. So can I leave?"

"That's for you to decide with your father and . . . guardian. I think you can really benefit from a few more days here. I want to help you during this stay in hospital so that you never need to return here again." He holds up my crazy-map.

But Balder doesn't understand the stakes. He doesn't know about the wolf. About how the ward is bringing us face-to-face, forcing a confrontation that doesn't need to happen. A showdown when I've never felt weaker. My mother can't even hold it back. If Balder knew, he'd keep me here for even longer and that would be worse.

. . . "I don't want people to know I'm here."

"Milly, mental illness is very, very common. It's nothing to be ashamed of. Were you ashamed of your mother for having cancer?"

. . . "That wasn't her fault."

"And this is not your fault either."

I swallow. *Mental illness, mental illness, mental illness.*

"Can you tell me a bit about your parents, about your stepmother?" he asks.

. . . "Okay, well, my dad isn't around much. He's in sales and has to travel all the time. My mom was a stay-at-home mom— that made her crazy . . . sorry, I didn't mean *crazy* crazy. But I'm an only child. She had so much time, so everything had to be perfect, and she did everything she could to make sure I had everything I needed and was, like, the safest kid in the whole world. She was pretty amazing, I guess. Then she got breast cancer when I was twelve and died really quickly, faster than normal."

I flush.

"And what about Adriana?"

. . . "She's a total bitch. I mean, she says she's trying to help, but she doesn't really care about me and is just annoyed by my presence. I know she's trying only to impress my dad. If I don't do what she wants, she flips out."

"All right, Milly, we'll help you work through some of these issues."

What issues—aside from the need for Adriana to disappear?

"Often we have some mistaken beliefs that are created by our familial relationships. The workbook will help us uncover them. You did a great job on the worksheet I gave you. Soon we can begin working on lowering those ratings."

. . . "There's a Halloween dance at school Friday. I want to go."

He smiles. "That gives us something to work toward. Let's see how the next twenty-four hours go with the goal of rewarding yourself with the dance, if you achieve a milestone we set together."

I nod, feeling like I've at least won something. He pauses, checks my lips to determine if I'm counting and have something more to say, and then continues. "I'd like you to take a look at the workbook. We give it to all our anxiety disorder patients and in it are some exercises. To start, I'd like you to fill out the one I've marked off with purple tabs."

Anxiety disorder. He thinks I have an anxiety disorder. Vanet was right.

Following his pointed finger, I can see small purple tabs marking off a couple pages in the book. Other tabs are yellow and green.

I shrug; he can't make me do anything. And he checks my lips again.

"Great. Now, I'm going to ask a few more questions. Why do you count?" he asks.

The wolf. I can picture it tracking the wingless fairy and me through the woods, skulking by the side of the cottage. . . . "Thank you for waiting to see if I wanted to talk. Conversations can be all messed up otherwise. Why do I count? Because something bad will happen, if I don't. Something terrible."

A part of me wants to tell him about the wolf. But I already know what he'll think—that I'm crazy, and then he really will drug me and my head will be too fuzzy to use my magic count and the wolf will have triumphed.

"What will happen?" His pen is dancing over his clipboard, and he doesn't look up with each question.

. . . "I dunno." I'm shaking my head. "Terrible things, anywhere." It's not smart even to talk about this sort of thing.

"You mean terrible things like earthquakes and volcanic eruptions, for instance?" He meets my eyes.

I shrug. *How does he know?*

. . . "Maybe to my friends, maybe anywhere and to anyone," I say.

"Why one hundred? Why not ten?"

That's the magic, the spell; the wolf's banished by a hundred, but he seems to expect a specific reason. . . . "One hundred percent. If I count to one hundred, there's a one hundred percent chance that nothing bad will happen. If I count to ten, there's a ninety percent chance that something bad will happen."

He nods. At least that seems to add up.

"Would you try something for me?" he asks. "Would you try counting to ten next time? Ten out of ten on a test is one hundred percent, right?"

I raise my eyebrow to show I think he's crazy. He doesn't understand this at all.

"Okay, how about ninety-nine?"

. . . "Do you want a one percent chance of dying today?" I ask. "I mean, a one percent chance that you'll be hit by a car, have a heart attack, be struck by lightning?"

He's smart enough to know this is a rhetorical question and doesn't reply, but I still need to count.

. . . "No, you wouldn't. So why would I want to take a risk like that?"

He purses his lips. "Do you really believe that you cause these terrible things to happen?"

I shrug. I don't, but I'm the only one who can stop them from happening.

"These automatic thoughts that come with a wave of anxiety are your OCD, your Obsessive Compulsive Disorder. Next time you have a thought like—'Something terrible will happen if I don't count'—I want you to identify it and say to it, 'You're just my OCD talking.'"

He says it as if it's a trivial matter. What he doesn't know is that me and my OCD, we're real close. Mama taught me never to talk to wolves.

"We're going to give you the weapons and training so you can fight this thing."

My bow and arrows. I smile despite myself and lean closer. Here's a language I understand.

When I don't say anything, he continues, "How are you enjoying the other patients?"

. . . "Enjoying? I'm enjoying it like I enjoy watching the

circus. These people are crazy. Pig's lying about everything. So is Vanet. Peter's the only person being real. One chick won't even wake up. Wesley, he barely speaks he's so depressed, perhaps not unusual for a guy who wears that much eyeliner. And Red, well I can understand why Red's in here, she clearly has some issues to work through, even if I don't know why yet."

"Everyone's in here for very different reasons, and they all have very different needs," Doctor Balder says.

He's stopped his scribbling and I guess the interview is over. With my counting, the whole thing took an hour, even though I bet we covered less than half of what he would have wanted.

After my meeting with him I'm bored, not interested in doing crafts with Tink or socializing, so I have a shower. I slide the bar on the door from "Vacant" to "In Use." It doesn't seem to matter. As soon as the jet of water hits the tiles, Vanet keeps "accidentally" trying to come in.

"Occupado!" I shout.

"Don't you have to count to shut a door?" he asks after I shove it back closed.

. . . "No, idiot, just to hop through it. Whatever you're taking, they need to increase the dosage." He gives up on his fourth attempt to see me naked.

At least he steers clear of my changing. My room's in sight of the nursing station, and Vanet's not allowed in. I slip into an *I love NY* T-shirt and a pair of jeans. No one else is in the room except Sleeping Beauty. I pick up my book of tales, the cloth binding warm beneath fingertips chilled from the shower. I open it to the first page and count the words, knowing where I'll end. At the word *wolf*. The hundredth word. A nutty scent wafts from the pages as I turn to the hundredth page, which begins, *There once was a girl who was the wolf's coveted meal.* Why do I count to one hundred? Because that's the magic.

I turn the page to a short tale, hoping for some new magic, even though I've read the book a hundred times.

There once was a girl who wandered into the woods on her sixth birthday. Everyone who met her, loved her, and her mother loved her most of all. So when she was found killed by a wolf, the whole town mourned for a week. But not a day went by that the mother didn't visit the little girl's grave and sob as she left flowers. At night the mother cried herself to sleep, and all through the day, small things that the little girl had loved brought tears to the mother's eyes. On the little girl's seventh birthday, the little girl appeared to her mother, who cried in the kitchen baking her daughter's favorite cake. The little girl said, "Please, Mother, I cannot rest for all your crying. Please stop."

Seeing that her daughter could not rest for her grief, the mother stopped her tears and only lit a candle for each year thereafter.

Suck it up. Let go and move on. Fairy tales make it look easy.

I snap the book closed. Beauty turns in her sleep.

There's something freeing about talking to the comatose. When talking, if I pause too long, I have to count again, but if I can get it right, I can speak without counting for a long time.

. . . "Hi, Beauty." She is certainly pretty in a delicate kind of way. "Why so sleepy? Waiting for your prince charming? I wouldn't wait. Those boys are fickle. I mean, could you imagine dating Vanet?" I chuckle and that definitely counts as a pause, and so I count again. I want to talk to Bill so badly it hurts, but he won't be home for an hour, so talking about him is the next best thing.

. . . "I have a date for the dance, if you're wondering. Dances aren't real dates, I guess. They rank with going to a movie. At least I hope we're going to the dance. His name's Bill—I know, Milly and Billy, ha-ha, but he really is cool. Black, dense hair, awesome body, plays tennis and runs a lot. He's a popular guy. I don't know what he sees in me, especially with my counting and all. What's awesome is he doesn't expect me to talk much, so we're a perfect match.

"So far we've seen two movies, tried to play tennis, and went to a noisy party where I never had to bother counting to talk. This will be our fifth not-real date. I don't really like the movies, but going with Bill makes me feel safe. Like the dance: without him I don't think I'd go, not by myself. Maybe he'll figure me out soon. Luckily I don't have to count before we kiss." I smile and start counting again.

. . . "I want to dance with him. I bet he's good, though, and I dance like an ostrich. It sucks when your stepmother dances better than you do. Twelve months after my mom died, she moved in. It's been two years and counting. Counting . . . ha-ha. So what's with the IV?"

I check the empty bag and choke back a cry. I know the name of the drug labeled on it. My mom was on it once. Beauty is undergoing chemotherapy. She has cancer.

When I look back, she's staring at me.

"Jesus says I'm healed," she says, eyes moving all over the place in their sockets.

. . . "Looks like the hospital isn't so sure Jesus got it all," I say.

Her eyes clear, and she seems to spot the IV port in her arm for the first time. She screeches and starts clawing at the needle.

It pulls out of her arm, blood smearing across her wrist. I'm counting like mad and finally clue into the red button on the wall and slam my fist into it. Beauty has already pretty much tired herself out by the time Nurse Abby and Stenson rush in, followed by Balder. In a minute, Beauty's sedated and Nurse Stenson's charting.

. . . "She's refusing treatment, right?" I ask.

Doctor Balder draws a deep breath and then returns to check his patient's pulse. And I think I get it. Beauty believes Jesus has healed her already. If she is healed, then to her the IV is renouncing His gift. Or at best filling her body with toxic chemicals for no reason.

Christ, I really don't belong here.

Chapter 13

While I was in my meeting with Doctor Balder, the teaching aide dropped off my course work from yesterday, plus what the teachers plan to cover the rest of the week. A stack of paper teeters on my desk. There's no way they will cover anywhere close to this much. I bet the teachers looked at what they had actually planned to cover, were embarrassed, and so tripled it. Except for my math teacher, he doesn't need to triple anything. Or maybe they know something I don't, that I'll be in here longer than the doctor's telling me.

Why don't adults tell kids everything? Why hide things? Sometimes I wonder whether my mom knew about her breast cancer long before she told me. So instead of having all those nights of arguments, I could have known she was dying. I could have helped her.

Breaking the truth slowly just means telling lots of little lies to avoid one big reality. I bet Adriana has had a conversation with Balder that went something like:

Don't worry, ma'am, she'll be here for a month, maybe four. She's good and mixed up. I'll give her so many diagnoses that her head will spin. And if she isn't sick, I'll be sure to make her sick within the week.

And then Adriana asked: *What about the dance, good, silver-templed doctor?*

That's when they both started laughing at the shared joke of me ever making it to the dance.

I like the concept of the dance. No one talks at a dance, not really. It's too loud in the school gym. And what else, other than chips and punch, is there to eat and drink? I'd be normal for the night, communicating in nods, smiles, and hand waves, swaying to the music.

I sit down at my desk and put my new workbook on top. I can see that Pig has a copy of it too amongst her clutter of papers and books. Other kids have scratched things into the desk's surface. Swearing, names and dates, silly faces, penises, the usual, plus some biblical scripture, death threats, and images of what looks like a hanging doctor or nurse. And a wolf. Just the head this time, as if its body is stuck through a knot in the wood. I don't remember this and wonder if it's new. I peer into the room's shadows, but nothing moves. Hair lifts at the back of my neck.

I try to start some math, but I can feel the eyes of the wolf under the pages, so I take a pen and scribble over it. It only serves to remind me of how it hides in the trees, waiting for me to slip off the path. I etch at the wood, covering every inch until I can't make it out. But it's still there. Underneath. In its den. My stomach clenches. It's my OCD, I tell myself. But just thinking that doesn't seem like much of a weapon.

Maybe I can use the workbook. Maybe if it seems like I'm

trying, Balder will let me get the hell back to home, where it's safe.

Some doctor has written a blurb on the cover: "The first anxiety workbook written in a language teens can really dig. Rock-on!"

Dig? Rock-on? Seriously? I bet it was written in the sixties.

I turn to the purple tab.

So, you've got a problem. People probably think you're wiggin' out, am I right? What a drag. Don't be bummed. I'm here to help you fix it. The first thing you need to decide is what groovy looks like.

Oh, my, god, it might as well be written in a different language.

Answer the following:

What changes will help you get your groove back?

What does groovy look like?

How will groovy change your relationships with your steady, your old man, or old lady?

Draw a picture of a gnarly life:

There's a big space where I'm supposed to draw. I burst out laughing.

When I stop, I get down to filling in blanks. How to become groovy? That's pretty simple. Stop the wolf. Kill it. If the wolf's gone, I can stop counting. Stop hopping. Stop being so nervous about everything. Stop fighting with Adriana, although I can't stop her from acting like an idiot. Stop having nightmares. Stop the wolf. Yeah, pretty much sums it up. Gnarly.

Groovy is this magical world where I can have a conversation without pissing off everyone around me. Where I actually talk to people rather than veer away when I see them coming. No wonder people call me stuck-up.

What's a steady? I'm going to assume it means boyfriend. How would my relationship change with Bill? I'd talk a lot more. But maybe he likes girls with problems. Would he be my boyfriend if I wasn't such a loser? Not that he's a loser, but would we be compatible?

How would things change with my dad? He'd worry less. It must be hard for him knowing I'm in the hospital and bummed and wiggin' out. I bite my knuckles to suppress a giggle. My relationship with Adriana would sure change. She likes how weak I am. It makes her look strong.

I skip the blank where I'm supposed to draw something and reread what I wrote.

Maybe I do have a problem. I mean, look at all the parts of my life affected by my counting. By the wolf.

It's my OCD . . . .

I glance at the black square, the buried wolf, and squint at it. Then I turn back to the blank area. I draw a picture of stick-me. The girl has stringy brown hair and bangs trimmed to fall just above green eyes. She's skinny, but then it's a stick girl. Then I give her a cap like Robin Hood might have worn and a quiver of arrows and bow. At her stick-hip I draw a fat hunting blade. After, small as I can, I rewrite the hunting license Vanet gave me and place it in the stick-hunter-me's hand.

I open the book of tales to page one hundred and read from halfway down.

Each day, the wolf crept closer, and grew bolder, and the magic of the spell grew weaker. The girl had to learn new magic, darker and more difficult magic. The dark magic drew the wood closer until the path overgrew with thorns and no new magic could protect her from the wolf.

That day the girl sharpened a hunting knife; she shouldered a quiver of arrows and strung a bow of yew. That day the girl gave up her magic and hunted the hunter.

Gave up her magic. She had no choice. She had no choice, because the Dark Wood became too strong. The wolf too ferocious.

But where are my real weapons? I can call out the wolf, but what then?

Pig enters. She scratches at her head, sighing deeply. "Anyone got a match?" she asks. "Just kidding. Don't go calling the nurses on me."

Pig slumps into her chair, rolls her bald head to me, and then huffs.

I shrug.

"When's your birthday?" she asks and then waits.

. . . "Friday, actually." I'd forgotten. "I'll be sixteen. I can drive. Sweet, sweet, crazy sixteen."

"Oh, nice, I've been sixteen for almost two years and the only car I've been in is a cop car." The thought seems to upset her because she starts banging her fist against the table. "Sorry." Pig's eyes flick to the ceiling. "Nerves. Getting out soon, end of my sentence is Saturday."

. . . "Congratulations," I say, but wondering if she's really ready to leave. She's more twitchy than Red. "You must be excited."

Her head lolls back and forth. "No, no, no," she says. "Not excited."

We sit in silence for a bit. It lets me count. "What happened, Pig?" I ask. "Why the fires? Is it like OCD and you can't stop yourself?"

She looks me up and down and then picks my book of tales off the table. "Let me tell you a little fairy tale.

"Once there were three little piggies who had to leave home. The momma piggy used to beat the pulp out of the girl piggy. And the daddy piggy beat up the two boy piggies. The piggy parents were gender-specific beaters, see? Momma piggy would never beat her baby boys, and daddy would never beat his girl. Even psychos have boundaries." She shudders, and I clench my hands to forestall a shiver of my own. My eyes are watering. I know far too well what she's really saying. "So the three little piggies left together. The little piggies couldn't do it each on their own, but together they could escape. But they didn't stay together. They didn't have much money, and no one wants to have to protect a sister piggy.

"The first little piggy, let's call him Jess. Jess found a bus shelter that he used as a home until a pack of wolves came and pounded his ass. He joined the wolves for protection. That lasted a year before the sister piggy had to identify him at the butcher.

"The second little piggy was the eldest. Call him Andy. He took his sister to a shelter for homeless piggies, but his money was stolen and he wanted to pimp out his sister piggy, so she ran. So the first piggy didn't find any help with the wolves. And the second piggy didn't get help from the shelters. So the third little piggy had to protect herself."

She stares at me as if to catch my reaction, but I go dead neutral, even though I suddenly want to run.

"So whenever this little piggy didn't feel safe, she'd light a fire. At first it was little fires in garbage cans. While they burned, no one touched her money or stuff, not with all the police about.

No one dared touch her." She grimaced. "The bigger the fire, the more uniforms, the safer, the better. So, yeah, the fires got bigger."

. . . "Whoa."

"I wait for you to count and all I get is a whoa?" She keeps pulling at an eyebrow ring, hauling on it so hard that her skin tents up.

As I count, I nod. We stare at each other. This is Pig. Pig's never felt safe unless surrounded by the police. I understand why. Especially if she couldn't even trust her brothers. The third little piggy built her house out of fire. Pig has magic of her own. She has a weapon.

. . . "Sorry," I say. "I hope you find a home near a police station."

She laughs and lets the brow ring snap back. "How about you, what's got you counting up a storm?"

Suddenly, I don't want to talk anymore. Or rather, I don't want to talk about illness, or trauma, or magic. I want to hear about too much homework or what some chick said about some boy, or who cheated on whom. There's life and then there's too much life.

. . . "I—I'll tell everyone at group. Better to say it all at once, right?"

Pig's face sours. "No way. I tell you, you tell me."

I shake my head, and she squints.

"Do you even know?" she asks. "I didn't figure out why I lit fires for a year. Not really. Most secrets we hide even from ourselves."

. . . "Like fears."

"Like wolves."

. . . "I gotta make a call."

"Have it your way." She folds her arms across her chest and watches me leave.

It's not only to get away from Pig. I need to talk to Bill, and there's only a narrow window of time that he's home. As I approach the nursing station, I smile nervously at Nurse Abby and nod to the phone. She leans forward to hand it to me. Her dark eyes flick from me to the acute room hallway. She checks that the corridor's empty, then she sits back and returns to her work.

My shuffling steps echo as I move as far from the nursing station as the cord allows. It's bad enough that the nurses and doctors are trying to get into our heads and tell us what we must be feeling. It's like we're on the set of some bad reality TV show where the doctors are the producers and nurses are feeding us the script.

With the dial tone at my ear, I glance down the hall to the door. If there had been any scratches, someone has cleared the debris and replaced the tile. Could someone here be helping the wolf?

I count and then dial Bill. He picks up. I know he has tennis after school, but that's in half an hour.

"Bill," he says and of course, he doesn't know it's me. It's just some blocked number he's seeing. I'm counting, but he understands the system where I knock three times, so he'll realize I'm there.

"Milly?" he asks. "Milly, is that you?"

. . . "Yeah, it's me." I sigh relief. I feel as though I'm in a foreign country and making contact is a dose of home.

"Why are you whispering, Milly? You okay? Teachers are saying you're in the hospital, what happened?"

. . . "I fainted at gym," I say. "Right after you saw me." So much for alien abductions and fairy tales. Those are beginning to seem too close to the truth. I want to say more, a whole lot more, especially so he doesn't grow frustrated by the long pauses, but I can't. I want to tell him where I am. So that he can say it's okay, that it doesn't matter. Why do I need him to say it for me?

"Are you okay?" he asks.

I fight tears. . . . "Yeah, still in the hospital, though. I miss you so much."

"When are you coming home? What's wrong? I saw them collect homework for you."

So he knows I'm here for a while. Maybe he knows everything.

. . . "The dance, I'll be back for the dance. I hope."

There's a pause and I know he's expecting an answer to the question of, *What's wrong?* But I'm not ready to share that, even if it isn't my fault, even if it's common and no one should care. I know they do. *I do.*

"Maybe I can come see you?" he asks. It's sweet, but I can't imagine what Vanet would say to Bill. I laugh. "What's so funny?"

. . . "Nothing, I just miss you, but I don't want you to see me in here."

"It's good to hear you laugh. I haven't heard you laugh for a while." Funny, but it's true. I haven't been really happy lately, and today I laughed not just once but a whole bunch of times.

"So, you're like that girl in the tower, what was her name?"

Rapunzel.

"I forget," he continues. "But you're stuck there with a witch or something and all I can do is listen to you."

. . . "I could let down my hair."

"That's the one, yeah, you could let down your hair and I could climb it."

I press the receiver tighter to my ear, as if that will bring us closer. . . . "That would hurt, but thanks for offering to be my knight in shining armor."

"No other knights there, huh?" He doesn't wait for a response, saying, "Listen, tennis, I gotta run."

. . . "Talk later," I say.

"For sure." He hangs up. I keep the phone to my ear. Once we sat in silence for an hour listening to the other's breathing, nothing needing to be said. I've never felt so close to anyone.

An automated voice tells me to please hang up.

I sigh and then squint. I can see the nursing station phone. Nurse Abby's on it. I end the call and the nurse hangs up too. At the same time. Was she listening in on my call?

I take a few steps toward the station. Nurse Abby winks at me from her chair before taking back the handset and returning to the charts.

Chapter 14

I can't help but think I've caught Nurse Abby at something. She leaves her nursing station to stand in gray Mary Janes and her black raven shirt.

"Peter?" she shouts down the hall.

I hear the smash of the remaining interview room mirror.

When I peer around the corner of the nursing station, Peter is being dragged into his dorm room by two red-faced orderlies. Only one orderly returns.

What I said to Doctor Balder is true. I like Peter, because he's not trying to manipulate me in any way. He doesn't care why I'm here or what my illness is. He's also been left out of pretty much every situation I've seen and deserves a friend. It's funny, because Peter's embraced his fairyness and everyone's trying to convince him otherwise.

Maybe I don't need to fight my wolf, but to embrace it. Give myself over to it. Am I not a feral creature at heart? Didn't my ancestors feel their blood pump as they hunted? Haven't I felt that as I clutched the back of Billy's skull and kissed him? Didn't I once know that feeling when I scored a goal or hoop? My book has another tale about a girl who embraced her wolf. It went like this:

There once was a girl who had run away from home because she did not like the man her father had ordered her to marry. Penniless and starving, she sheltered in the dark wood, where she met a man who told her that he would give her gold and a home if she would only prove her innocence to him. Without noticing the man's cloven hooves that marked him as the devil, she agreed and in doing so proved her innocence. But the man had one further condition, that she wear a wolf skin for eight years and not wash, comb her hair, or cut her nails. If she died during that time, her soul would be his, but if she survived, then he would give her all that she asked.

Not having any money or other prospects, the girl agreed, and for eight years the girl wandered the world growing ever filthier, her nails growing into claws, and the grime coating her so thick that those who passed her ran in fear that she was a real wolf. Thrice the huntsman tracked her, and thrice she sang a sweet song to convince him she was no wolf, but a girl. But on the very last day of her trial, her singing couldn't be heard over the baying of dogs and a band of four huntsmen shot her until she neared death. Seeing their crime, they killed themselves in shame.

As she lay dying, the day turned and with the dawn, so did the devil come again as promised. The girl demanded that he save her life, and he did, plucking the arrows from her and closing the wounds. And then she demanded he make her rich and he did. Cleaned and now beautiful, she asked if he was angry that she had won. He replied: "I may have lost one soul, but I have gained four more."

I think it has something to do with the law of unintended

consequences. Embrace your wolf—everyone dies. But embracing your inner fairy is different from the wolf. I want to ask Peter why he's afraid of his wolf.

I move a little closer to Peter's room. Nurse Abby has returned to her station, and she clinks around in cupboards until finally clacking past me holding a pill in a cup. This time when the door opens, I see Peter strapped to the bed with the orderly pressing down with one hand on a buckle.

Five minutes later they both come out, and I wait until the nurse and the orderly start chatting. Counting, I head for Peter's door. We're not allowed in patient rooms other than our own, but I don't care. What can they do that's worse than being in here in the first place?

When I enter, Peter's bawling. He turns to me. His head lifts off the mattress, but there's a dull sheen to his stare, even for him. Thick leather straps hang from the bed. He's no longer in restraints.

. . . "Shh . . . Peter . . . it's okay. Shh . . ." And he tries to quiet himself, lower lip quivering as great tears squeeze from his eyes. Finally, he looks up at me expectantly.

. . . "Do you have any brothers and sisters?" I ask. "Anyone that comes to see you?"

He swallows and nods. "Two old brothers. Real old. They take me on holidays. Sometimes Charlie's turn and sometimes Nico's turn. I like Nico best, but I have to wait his turn."

They trade him. He's a burden to them. He's sweet, but perpetually a child. I don't ask after parents; they're not around.

"In the rec room, you said you've seen a wolf."

He pales. "The wolf," he says. "Pig told me. It wants to eat me. They keep him in alone, all tied up, but the wolf knows a way."

I'm a bit disappointed. It's another rumor spread by Pig.

. . . "Did the wolf tell you to jump out that window?"

His expression says that I must be crazy.

"No, the witch, the witch tells me to jump."

. . . "Who is the witch? Where is she?"

He glances around the room as if the witch might be here listening and then whispers, "She's in the mirrors."

That explains it. If a witch could watch and speak through any mirror, that would mess a guy like Peter up.

He sits forward and I stumble back. He's just so big and strong, the restraints dangle loose, and here I am, alone with the guy.

His face squinches. "Fairies don't hurt people. I'm a good fairy."

In my book of tales, fairies are pretty darn nasty. . . . "Sorry, Peter, I'm jumpy."

I consider Peter. It's not that I feel sorry for him, that's not fair to Peter. In his own way, he's doing pretty well, and maybe it's because no one's giving him any credit that I'm feeling bothered. No one wants him in their circle. If he wants to be a fairy, why not make him the best fairy ever? Why not help him to embrace it?

. . . "Of course you are a good fairy," I say and add quickly before I need to count again, "Do you want to look even more like a fairy? A great fairy?" His eyes light and he nods frantically. "You stay here and wait for me to come back. I'm going to make you the best fairy ever, but first I need a few things."

He nods.

. . . "Wait, okay?" I say. "You're safe from the wolf here."

I'm not convinced he'll stay put, but I sneak out of the room and hover by the door to the rec room counting.

No one's at the craft table when I dart inside to collect everything I could possibly need. Sparkles, glue, felt, cardboard, the most useless scissors I've ever seen, markers, anything and everything. Rottengoth's buried in a book; Pig must still be working on her homework, and Red probably joined her. Which leaves . . . .

"I want in," Vanet says, coming up from behind and tapping me on the shoulder.

. . . "In on what?" I ask.

"As a professional up-to-something person myself, I know you're up to something."

I stare at him, and I swear his eyes dance. . . . "We're going to dress Peter up like a proper fairy," I say.

"Makes sense," Vanet replies. "What do you want me to do?"

I glance again back through the door, but no one seems to care we have a craft project. . . . "We need to get this stuff into your room and make fairy things."

"You don't think they'd like us dressing Peter up like a fairy in here?"

. . . "Do they like anything you do?"

"Good point," he replies, "but we can't do it in the bedroom. The nurses check on us every fifteen minutes."

I hadn't thought of that. . . . "Okay, we'll have to do as much as we can here, and time it so we put on his makeup before they check again."

We set to it.

Vanet starts on a fairy crown while I make wings out of tape and newspaper.

"Told you I was a fairy godmother," Vanet says, holding up a golden cardboard circlet, which he somehow managed to trim neatly with the dull plastic scissors. "Let me know if you need any wishes granted."

The cost of help from Vanet is too high and too obvious.

. . . "I'd rather have shock therapy," I say.

"Wes swears by it, and I bet Wolfgang practically glows they've lit him up so many times," Vanet replies.

. . . "Do you know Wolfgang?"

He shakes his head. "No, but I've seen them take him down to ECT a bunch of times."

ECT. Electroconvulsive Therapy. It may work, but I'd rather pass.

I roll up a final piece of paper and fill it with sparkles before taping the larger end closed, leaving a tiny gap at the point—a fairy wand.

. . . "Bring the markers and paints," I say. "We go when we see the nurse do her next check."

I count to leave and indicate with my head for him to carry everything. It's his room so he can enter whenever he wants.

Three minutes later, Nurse Abby does her check and then moves on to 3A. I can only pass through the first door, so Vanet ducks into his room ahead of me.

Finally I'm through without being seen.

Vanet sits on a bed mounded with clothes. Peter has his fist up and shakes it at Vanet.

. . . "It's okay, Peter," I say. "He's helping dress you up like a proper fairy."

We're wasting valuable time.

"So you'll really fly," Vanet says.

Peter gives a little hoot of joy and lowers his arm.

. . . "Okay, I think this will go better if you hold still." Peter freezes, eyes wide. "Good, good, just like that. So, a fairy needs a crown for his hair." I place on his cropped head the crown Vanet made. "And sparkles on his skin and some makeup."

"While you're doing that, I can maybe do some cool tattoos," Vanet says.

"Wings, don't forget my wings," Peter adds.

The corners of his mouth have shot up in a wild grin. I paint on makeup while Vanet draws ropey vines over Peter's arms with markers.

. . . "When you're done with the tats, see if he's got anything fairyish to wear," I say.

Vanet chuckles. "Oh, he's got fairyish." He continues marking off hooked thorns and slender curls of offshoots.

I'm working blue, purple, and green into a kaleidoscope of heavy eye shadow. Peter's lips will be a pale blue. But I'm working too fast and the result is garish, so I color in all of his cheeks, chin, forehead, and nose a sunshine yellow. With some blending . . . there. Rainbow fairy.

. . . "Vanet, that's so amazing," I say. Vanet's tattoos are a wilderness of thorny vines, carefully inked and with the hint of menace in their shadows. The cast he transformed into the leg and talons of an eagle. Maybe he is the fairy godmother. He's the only person I've ever met who actually seems to believe anything is possible.

He peers at my work. "Bright," he says. "Very bright."

"I'm a fairy," Peter replies.

. . . "I'll get the wings," I say.

"I see?" Peter asks.

"Not yet, brother fairy," Vanet says. "Are you a king or a queen?"

"King," Peter says. "Fairies are hard to tell, girl or boy."

Vanet holds up a yellow tank top for approval and some Bermuda shorts.

"Yeah, yeah," Peter says.

He helps Peter dress, and after, I slip great loops of tape over the newspaper and then over his shoulders, attaching the wings.

The wings suck in comparison to Vanet's crown and tattoos, but it's close to room check, and I'll be caught in here if I take any more time to decorate the paper with feathers.

"What if I fall?" Peter asks.

"But what if you fly," Vanet replies.

. . . "Magic wand." I hand Peter the wand I made.

He flicks it and sparkle dust shoots from its tip. Peter gasps.

"Careful with that, fairy dust is hard to come by," Vanet says.

But Peter's head is scanning for something. "Mirror, mirror, on the wall. I'm a fairy, I'm a fairy," he says and dances out of the room on his cast's talons; fairy dust spritzes everywhere.

Vanet's eyes shine with fun. "That was a nice thing to do," he says.

. . . "Who says he's not a fairy?" I ask. And I feel a little wild. A little free.

"You better get out of here," he says.

That's what I'm counting for.

Chapter 15

When we leave the room, I expect to hear sounds of shouting, maybe laughter, but there's nothing.

Vanet pops into the shower, pretty sure it's to hide, but it's not like we did anything really wrong. The washroom's marked "In Use" already. So to hide I'd have to join Vanet, but he'd get the wrong idea.

It's then that I turn and see—the door leaving the ward is propped open. I peer out. A huge newsprint-winged fairy thumps down the hall on his eagle-talon cast. The lunch lady walks out of the cafeteria pushing her big trolley of trays and kicks the doorstop away as she passes into the hallway. It begins to shut.

Peter's loose.

I'm counting to race after him. But this is bigger than me. Fear burns through my stomach.

It's my OCD.

It doesn't help!

I run for it, but I only make it to sixty before the door closes. At the end of the hall, Peter has disappeared through a fire exit.

Peter escaped. I check the nursing station, but no one's there. I can't decide what to do.

. . . "Nurse?" I call, but cackles of laughter erupt from the rec room and cover the sound. There is no one at the nursing station.

Why would Peter go? *The mirror.* He needed a mirror to see himself. And what else did he say about the mirror? *The witch tells me to jump.* The wicked witch. *What if I fall?*

I race to the rec room door. All the staff is inside except Nurse Abby. Tink and Doctor Balder's paddles are a blur as the ping-pong ball whizzes back and forth. Staff and patients cheer another point for Tink. She's *really* good.

I'm through the door and rush over to knock the ball away. A calm smile spreads across Doctor Balder's face.

. . . "Peter's escaped," I shout. "He went through the fire exit at the end of the hall. I'm sorry."

The doctor swivels to Stenson. "Call the code." Then he sprints out the door. We all follow.

Nurse Abby comes out of the washroom to a crowd of patients clustered in the hall, all watching the door close behind Doctor Balder.

"What's happened?" she asks.

"Code gray," blares the overhead PA. "Code gray."

The nurse, her face now matching the color of the code, races to her station.

I slide down the wall and wait on the cool linoleum floor.

Rottengoth, Pig, Tink, and Red mill in the hallway as if not sure what to do. Vanet peeks from the shower door, straightens, and then mingles with the crowd.

"What's going on, what's happening?" he asks, all innocent.

Twenty minutes pass before Peter is dragged, wingless and wandless, back through the doors. He's bawling and looks more clown than fairy.

"I'm a fairy. I'm a fairy," he cries and then, seeing where they're headed, digs his heels in and twists around. The security staff—four of them now—lift him bodily and carry him through to the room that I stayed in when I first arrived. Nurse Abby follows them, gripping a needle like a SWAT officer holds a handgun. The door closes.

"Found him on the roof," I hear someone say.

"Group, everyone." Tink's voice breaks.

Even Red doesn't try to avoid group. Everyone crowds back into the rec room. Another car crash to gawk at.

"*Everyone* to group," Stenson orders as I still sit in the empty hall.

I'm grateful that Tink's taking group, but suspect it's only because Stenson's tied up dealing with the mess I created.

I sit between Rottengoth and Red.

"So," Tink says, her lips straining between smile and grimace. "That was exciting. Now who dressed Peter up?"

Right down to business. This is serious Tink. There's silence. Vanet's dark eyes bore into mine and then shift to my lips. He twitches his head in a tiny no. But I only hasten my count.

. . . "I—"

"I did it," Vanet interrupts me, and I have to restart my count. There's no hint of remorse in his response. "See, Peter's a fairy. He really is, right? He prances around. He says he's a fairy. When he's in proper fairy clothes, he looks like one. It seemed only fair to help him out. That's what life's about, right? Helping people? Being fair to fairies."

I'm not sure how Vanet makes these leaps, but I wish I could too.

"Earlier," Pig points at Vanet, "he told Peter he'd see the land of fairies, if he kept jumping off of buildings."

"Also true," Vanet agrees.

"Why would you do such a thing?" Tink asks.

"You don't think we should help people achieve their dreams?" Vanet replies, hand over his chest.

"How do you think you were helping him?" Tink tries again.

"I told you. He's a king. Of the good fairies at least. A king fairy should look like one."

Tink's mouth tightens and her strained smile finally folds. "Why might you think telling Peter he's a fairy could be a bad thing?" The question is for all of us. I'm counting to speak, but Vanet meets my eyes and shakes his head again.

He *wants* to take the fall for this.

"Because he's going to keep jumping out of buildings!" Pig screams, her face pink.

"Darwin Award winner," Red agrees.

"Okay, so he may hurt himself. Why else might it not be healthy? Vanet thought he was God when he first arrived. Why was it important that he realize that he's Vanet, not God?" Tink doesn't sound like her true self and I know why. She's angry. She would be at me, too, if she knew.

"Because we should be ourselves," Rottengoth says.

"Good, Wes," Tink replies, her shoulders releasing their tightness just a smidge. "We should be ourselves."

"What if we don't like ourselves?" Rottengoth says back. "Shouldn't we try to change things we don't like?"

"Of course," Tink says. "Things we can change."

"Like if I'm not fairy enough, I should put on wings and—"

"Vanet," Tink scowls. "If you're to participate in group, you will respect it." She no longer tries to hide her fury. "What just happened was very dangerous, and it happened because an individual took it upon himself to challenge the treatment regime of another patient. Peter was improving, little by little, but—" Tink lifts her hands to the ceiling in exasperation. Her eyes fill with tears, and she clenches her jaw in her effort to control them. "He could have died. He was on the roof."

"Someone shouldn't have left the door open," Red says. "Nothing would have happened if the door was shut."

Tink flushes, smooths her pants, and uses the shoulders of her pale green blouse to clear her eyes. I can't help but think the blouse is something Peter would love to wear. Her smile is back, false as it is.

"Wesley, you said something interesting. Why did you say you didn't like yourself?" she continues.

Somehow Rottengoth seems even skinnier as he shifts on his bony butt. Ear-stretchers have opened his lobes to the gauge of a quarter.

"I don't have any friends and my parents—they hate me." He stares at his hands and brings the palms together and apart like they're doing push-ups.

"What evidence do you have to support that?" Tink drops into the same Socratic method Stenson uses. Rottengoth gazes at her as if she must be nuts. "How do you know your father hates you?" Tink asks.

He draws a deep breath. "We'll be doing stuff, okay, fixing

something and I won't do it right and he'll be like *why can't you just*... he always says that... *why can't you just*... and then shakes his fist. After that he'll ignore me."

"Maybe fixing things makes him angry," Tink suggests.

"Your dad's a jerk," Vanet says, but Rottengoth shakes his head.

"That's the problem though, he's not. He's pretty nice. I've got this little brother, and he's good at every sport and my dad, he ruffles his hair all the time, musses it up and gives him these little hugs all the time. Calls him Tiger. I'm not saying I want anyone mussing my hair or hugging me, but... maybe he doesn't hate me. Maybe he just doesn't care. Maybe that's worse." He sighs, shoulders seeming to droop to his hips. "What's wrong with me, then? If my parents don't care about their kid, what's that say about me?"

Tink glances toward the door and she looks super uncomfortable, like she's taken this all a little too far.

"They care," she says lamely. "They care." With a quick smile adds, "It's been a very eventful morning, why don't you wash up for lunch?"

I'm left a little stunned by Wes's comments. My mom always used to say to me, *why can't you just*... too. It was usually when I was doing something that scared her, like sitting too close to the television, or walking too close to the side of the curb, or not wearing my hat in the sun. *Why can't you just sit still?* Sometimes I wonder if she'd have preferred I stayed indoors and read my book of tales all day. Even when I did stuff, I was never quite good enough anyway. *You could have done better.* She really wanted the best for me.

Tink drifts away. I'm counting to leave, but no one else moves to the door.

"That was hilarious," Red says to Vanet.

"The part where Wesley's parents hate him?" Vanet asks, and it's one of the first times I think I've seen him serious.

"At least he has parents who are alive, who are nice," Pig replies.

Rottengoth's face drops.

Then Vanet bursts out laughing. "Sorry, sorry, as if I care."

Chapter 16

There's a story in the book of tales that I'm not sure I *get.*

A millwright had two daughters old enough to be married. The first daughter married a pig farmer because she felt they would always have food to eat. The second daughter married a huntsman because she felt they would always have warm furs to wear.

As time went on, each daughter had many children and during times of plenty, both were happy with their husbands. Lean years were very different, however. During drought years, the daughter who married the pig farmer was happy for what little they had even if they were cold some evenings. But during times when animals were scarce, the daughter who married the huntsman railed against her hunger and sent her husband back out to find food to feed them.

One day, the starving huntsman left to hunt and never returned, likely eaten by ravenous wolves.

With nowhere else to go, the daughter who married the huntsman turned to her sister, the pig farmer's wife, for help. The pig farmer's wife welcomed her into their family and, despite the added mouths to feed, the pig farmer and his wife were thankful for what they had even if some days they were cold and hungry.

Don't nag? Is that the moral? Well, sister number two was definitely a total bitch.

Peter's not at lunch. Before me is my half-empty can of Ensure and a goey slab of lasagna. Everyone's busy eating, and the clatter of spoons and forks on trays rings out.

"Maybe they're feeding Peter through a tube in his stomach," Vanet says.

"Don't be gross," Pig replies. "Milly has a hard enough time eating without that crap."

My vision swims. It's like when I fainted at gym all over again. I grip the table to steady myself.

My mother had a feeding tube near the end. When they removed it, she spent another week dying. She almost died a dozen times before she finally went. We were all there for the tube removal, when my dad finally asked for the nurse to remove it and the IV lines, so that my mom could die quietly. But she didn't die right away. And death isn't quiet.

My mom's close friends and her brother were all there that first day, on deathwatch. But the group got smaller with every additional day. Dad slept beside her, listening to her breathing. He would call me in whenever my mom's breaths went erratic or too shallow.

This is it, honey. This is it. Every time he said that. And his heart nearly broke every time.

At first this cold feeling would rush through me, bracing me for the worst. But after a while, it was like that story about the boy who cried wolf and the villagers who didn't show up when the boy truly needed them. I heard my dad talking to my mom's brother on speakerphone one time. My uncle said that he'd already said goodbye enough times. *Au revoir* was what he said, instead of goodbye.

I've heard that there's a moment at the very end when you wake and talk to those around you, and say *au revoir*. It wasn't like that with my mom. I wasn't even there. She died while I was sleeping over at a friend's house. That was before I had to count. My dad never even called; he slept through it too. If he had called, though, I'm not sure I would have come. Can you carry guilt for something that you might have done? What did the villagers think when they came upon the slaughter in the hills?

"Eat," Toadie tells me.

I used to like lasagna. Now everything tastes like sawdust mixed with wallpaper glue. In fairness, this is not my mother's lasagna, and hers was amazing.

. . . "I have to go to the washroom," I say.

"Not until an hour after eating," Toadie replies.

. . . "But I've only had one bite and some Ensure."

"You can hold it," Toadie says.

"Milly, what is the evidence of your needing to go to the washroom?" Vanet asks, mimicking Stenson perfectly.

. . . "I have a grumbling in my belly, and I'm pretty sure I've got a load destined for my pants if Toadie doesn't let me go," I reply.

Toadie appears confused.

"Yes, but are you looking at the whole picture?" Vanet asks.

. . . "Well . . . maybe not. I mean, the symptoms could mean that a blood vessel burst and I am bleeding out in my abdomen. Or I am about to give birth to an alien that is presently fighting to explode out of my anus."

"And are you being objective?" he asks.

. . . "I'm on a psych ward, how can I know?"

Toadie folds his arms and stares at the ceiling.

"Let me ask again, do you need to take a dump?" Vanet asks.

. . . "Yes, but only in a different dimension," I reply.

Vanet high-fives me.

Everyone else eats while I stare Toadie down, but he's not having it.

"The fairy thing was pretty crazy," Rottengoth says.

"That's nothing." Vanet shovels in a quarter of his meal in a single bite.

"What's the craziest thing you've done?" Pig asks the table.

"The craziest thing that I remember doing, or that people have told me I've done?" Vanet says. "When I get manic . . . ." He whistles.

"You're not manic now?" Pig asks.

"You kidding? This is totally normal, don't you think? I don't sound crazy, do I? Damn, this is boring. There's a reason bipolars skip their meds. Normal sucks."

"Craziest thing you've done, then, and you have to remember doing it," Pig replies.

"Okay, there was this chick—"

I'd been waiting for this and counting. "And it can't be about sex," I say.

He throws up his hands as if that severely limits his options, but soon recovers. "Wait, I've got one. My school has a cadet corps and it's really a bully boot camp. Know what I mean? It's filled with the big kids who are no good at sports, but still love bossing people around. In cadets they get to form teams of bullies and really pound on people." He shrugs. "People like me. I think the whole thing is stupid. Training to be soldiers, marching in bands and crap. Anyway, so one night they invite all of the cadet corps from around the region to this farm and they hold exercises. War games. Well, I and my friends decide to mess with the bullies a bit.

"Each cadet corps has a flag that they need to protect, so we decide to form a corps of our own and go capture their flags. Crash their party. So far so good, am I right? It all makes sense, but then we have too much peach schnapps—never drink it, worst hangover ever—anyway, we decide to make Molotov cocktails, so that we can take out fortifications, right?"

"This is crazy," Rottengoth says. "You made bombs?"

"Wait, wait, it gets better. We're sneaking up, and there's this commander taking a whiz while talking on his radio. We tackle him, blindfold him, tie him up, and gag him, and now we have his radio and know everything that's going on. This becomes important later after we throw the first cocktail to take out a protected bridge." He says this all matter-of-fact, as if they could hardly have done anything else. "Well, the war games turn from capture the flag into a manhunt. A field of dried cornstalks somehow ends up on fire. But we're still after their flags, so it's funny, because they're not protecting them anymore, they're starting to search for us while other people are putting out the fires. We just walk into each area and pick the flags off their poles. We know everything they're doing because of the radio and, by the time they figure that out, we're gone. I still have those flags over my bed—at home. And, you know what? That farmer grew the best corn in the country after the fire. Won first prize at some corn fest."

"I can't top that," I say and I can tell he isn't lying, not this time.

"Nobody died or anything," he adds.

"When it comes to setting things on fire, I can top any story," Pig says.

But Rottengoth raises his hand slowly and we all look over. "I have only one crazy story. I'm not a Satanist or anything, and I'm not part of a cult, but I did go to a weird ritual once. It was in an old warehouse with about a dozen people all wearing masks. Candles flickered everywhere and I chanted to try to raise a demon from Hell. That wasn't the really crazy part, though. This hooded girl brought a goat into the middle of the circle and it began to bleat as if it knew what was going to happen next. When they asked for volunteers to kill the goat, I told her that I knew how to handle a knife. She took me by the hand and I stepped into the circle. The goat was wandering around, pellets popping out of its butt like we were playing goat bingo—"

"Goat bingo, what's goat bingo?" Vanet asks, and Pig gives him a shot in the arm.

"Shut up," Pig says.

Rottengoth swallows and continues. "I grabbed it by the horn, hauled back and slit its throat. Didn't make a sound except for the blood splattering on the floor. I told myself that it was to put it out of its misery but the truth was, I wanted to. It was really easy, the blade slipped through . . . ." He glances down at his forearms and I can see all the scars; they're not the type you'd expect from a suicide attempt, lots of smaller ones. He shakes his sleeves down. I rub the gooseflesh from my arms.

"You're messed," Red says.

"You don't need ECT, you need an exorcism," Vanet adds. "Goths are crazy."

"Shut up. That's not Goth," Rottengoth says. "I told you. Besides, I didn't go again."

"Come on, Tiger. Did you drink its blood?" Vanet asks. "You can gain its powers, if you do that. If you drank the blood, it beats my crazy thing, otherwise I'd say tossing incendiary grenades at militant teenagers wins."

"Don't ever call me Tiger." Rottengoth jumps up, fists clenched. It's the most riled I've seen him.

"Who wants goat power?" Pig laughs. "The power to digest grass. The power to make annoying sounds. Maaa . . . maaaa . . . maaaa."

I wish I could believe in Satanism. If there are demons, then there are angels too. And maybe my mom really is watching me. Maybe she's forgiven me for not being there when she woke up in the dark, ready to say goodbye, and only found the wolf there to take her.

Au revoir, Mommy.

Toadie steps in between Vanet and Rottengoth. Lunch is over. We never did get to hear the craziest thing Pig's done.

I go back to my room to lie on my bed. When I walk in, a woman lifts her head from where she's hunched over Beauty. The woman continues whispering after I enter, but her eyes track me. Finally, she kisses a crucifix hanging on a chain around her neck. She was praying and now I can guess where Beauty got her belief that Jesus would save her.

"Hello," she says and I nod.

. . . "How is she?" I ask.

123

The woman smiles, a beaming, heaven-sent ray of light. Tears fill her eyes. "My daughter's going to be okay, she really is."

I wonder if it's the first time she's allowed herself that thought. Sure, I bet she'd hoped for her to be okay, prayed for it, but I can tell she believes it now. Seeing her beatific face, I try to recall ever seeing my mom like that, just so happy it oozed through her pores. I can't remember. It's hard losing your memory of someone you loved. And I did love her. She was strict at times, but when she was proud of me, I remember feeling her smile like a ray of light. That was when she was radiant. When I did everything right. It just didn't happen very often.

. . . "I'm happy for you," I say.

"Life's something you have to keep fighting for," she replies. "Never stop."

. . . "I won't," I reply. At first I take what she said at face value. Someone blabbing about the beauty of life, but then I wonder if there's more to it. A religious something. From Beauty's perspective, she's here because she believed in something her parents didn't like. She might be wrong, but no one's taken her side into account.

I glance back at Beauty and feel compelled to fight for her. To tell her side of the story, or at least as much as I can guess at.

. . . "Did you see it as suicide?" I ask and the woman frowns. "I mean, did you see her not taking the chemo as suicide, is that why you forced her to take it? You feared for her soul?"

Her fingers scrunch up the sheets.

"In a way," she replies.

I gather everything I need to say, because I don't think she'll give me another chance to count.

. . . "So she's here not because she's sick in the head, but because her soul is somehow at risk? How is that any better than her thinking Jesus will save her?"

She jerks to her feet and says, "He has. The difference is she's not dead." The woman strides out.

She wouldn't be the first person to mistake Jesus for the prince with true love's kiss.

Chapter 17

"Relaxation exercises!" Tink calls. Standing in the rec room doorway, she vibrates with energy. "SO excited, come on, come on. Vanet and Wes, move the couch; Pig and Red, you move the ping-pong table. Everyone take one of the yoga mats! We're going to RELAX!"

She fiddles with a small stereo and on comes the sound of waves crashing against a beach. "Ah, that's so nice."

It sounds to me like a tsunami disaster being endlessly repeated. This is not going to be relaxing. Red stands at the edge of her mat, doing her twitchy-shake thing. Vanet flops on the couch he moved against the wall.

"Vanet, grab a mat," Tink says.

"What? Are you saying I don't know how to relax? I'm so chill I can teach this."

"Chilling and mindful relaxation are very different things, come on, it'll be fun!"

Vanet shrugs and takes a position at the back. I know that he's hoping to check out my ass, but I suspect we'll be spending most of the time lying down so I don't bother moving away from where I've set up my mat.

"Yay." Tink hops from foot to foot.

I think she's extra excited because it's the first time I've seen everyone on the unit here. Even Peter made it, and he grins after me like I didn't almost kill him yesterday. Only Beauty's missing, and she doesn't need relaxation exercises. Rottengoth stands near Vanet, head already hanging low. Peter's jumping on one foot next to Rottengoth. Red's beside me in the front row, then Pig is on my other side with a smirk on her face.

"First we're going to learn how to breathe," Tink says.

Vanet draws in a long noisy breath and then squeaks out, "Help, I forget how to breathe, help."

Only Peter laughs.

"We are going to enter the moment," Tink continues. "We will exist in the moment without cares or worries of the world around us. Ready to be mindfully chill, Vanet? To chill on purpose?"

"Entering moment now," Vanet says like a robot.

"Good, let go of your hang-ups, let go of your fears, let go of every little thought in your minds," Tink says.

I frown and try to tune out her shrill little voice and stupid little ideas.

"Usually when you breathe, you only use the top part of your chest, but there's something called the diaphragm in the lower part. Everyone place your hand over your stomach. Good. Now breathe in and concentrate on trying to fill your stomach with air."

It's not possible to tune out a voice this annoying, so I comply and hold my stomach.

It takes a few tries, but eventually I can feel what she's talking about. It's weird to think I never knew of the bottom lung in my stomach.

"Take three deep breaths, you count the breath going in, being in, and going out," she says.

"Careful, Milly," Pig says. "Don't count to a hundred."

I can see by the smile on her face that she's not being mean and I nod back. Truth is, I feel a bit lightheaded, as if I'm not used to quite this much oxygen. Can you die breathing too much?

Tink motions for us all to lie on our mats. I collapse gratefully and stare at the ceiling. I hadn't noticed how stained the ceiling tiles were. Waves crash over me. Wow, for a second there I didn't even think about counting.

"This next part is called progressive muscle relaxation and you can do it sitting in a big chair or lying down like this. We're going to flex different muscle groups and then relax them. With each breath, feel yourself sinking deeper and deeper into the floor." Her voice has changed, hypnotic and low. "Draw in those stomach breaths.

"First, clench your hands into fists and hold them for three breaths . . . relax," Tink says. "Next, squeeze your biceps and flex your forearms."

She works her way up to our shoulders, telling us to squeeze, encouraging us to relax.

"Allow yourself to forget about your worries. Nothing will happen, nothing for the next twenty minutes."

Rottengoth begins to snore and we all giggle, but Tink ignores him.

"Wes wins," Vanet says. "He's the best relaxer."

"Be mindful of your breathing. If you have deep, even breaths that are easy, then you're doing it right," Tink says, and directs us to squeeze our eyes shut, to relax the lids, the eyeballs themselves, to let our jaws hang. It's weird, but every time I concentrate on something, I realize how tense it is. I close my eyes, pressing the eyelids together as hard as I can, and then I let go. My face smooths. I can't remember the last time it's ever felt this comfortable. Then I picture the folds of my brain and I shake them out, letting thoughts go, letting fears subside. I breathe.

I'm drifting off. I'm sinking into the floor.

"Go someplace safe. Let go. Let go. Let go."

I am bobbing on a raft on a lake. The sun bakes my back. The water laps against the dock and the boat's bumpers squeal every time a bigger wave shifts the hull. It's so warm; I can smell the sunlight. It's streaked my hair gold. I'm at my grandparents' cottage. My parents are both alive, but they're at home, and my grandparents are caring for me. I'm only eight, but they let me roam. To do as I please. To eat when I'm hungry, to sleep when I need to, just to be.

Tink wakes me with a nudge to my shoulder. "Next time try not to sleep. Mindful relaxation is a skill and you need to pay sharp attention. You need to . . . be . . . on . . . guard for SLEEP!"

I blink at her energy, and she flits away. The world rushes back, the walls of the Dark Wood menace, and with it the musty carpet smell.

For the rest of the day, I steer clear of activities, hoping to finish my homework and to catch Vanet alone. After dinner I finally corner him.

. . . "Ping-pong?" I ask.

"Seriously? I won the intergalactic championships at age twelve."

. . . "So school me."

"The last guy I schooled dislocated his shoulder," he says, but picks up a paddle.

. . . "I promise not to try so hard." After the first few serves, which neither of us can return, I ask, "Why did you say it was you who decorated Peter?"

He shrugs. "It was."

. . . "Yeah, but—" I glance to the door. It's empty. "Not only you."

The ball dances over the table and I manage to hit it back. We rally three hits. Although, I'm not sure we can call three a rally.

"You do want to go to the dance, right?" he asks. "With this . . . guy."

I hate private calls in public places.

. . . "Bill, but what does that have to do with anything?"

He palms the ball and holds it out. "Billy and Milly, right. The staff here has more power over you than you think. If you believe you can talk to your mom and they'll let you pop out of here whenever you like, then you do need to be schooled." His fingers curl around the ball. "Troublemakers don't get rewards."

. . . "Stepmom," I say.

"Whatever."

. . . "You took the blame, because you don't think I'll make it to the dance otherwise?"

He serves again. "That and the prospect of sexual favors."

. . . "As if." His return bounces high, and I slam it down, scoring. The ball lands on the couch. "Winner and new intergalactic champion!" I lift my arms.

"Your desire to play ping-pong is clearly a mischanneling of sexual frustration." He turns to dig around in the couch cushions for the ball. When he finds it, it's dented. And he flicks it over to me. Game over. I don't know why, but I pocket the wrecked ball. Vanet shrugs and starts to walk out. I still haven't thanked him.

. . . "Vanet?" I ask and continue right along so I don't have to count. He keeps on walking. His pockets bulge with what look like tennis balls. "Thanks, I feel bad about Peter. And about you taking the hit for it."

He gives me the thumbs-up as he passes through the door.

Vanet seems to have cooled a little. He's not as upbeat, not always *on* like he was when I first met him. Sometimes it was hard to understand where he was headed with a train of thought. But he's also less happy seeming, or maybe just less flirtatious.

I actually feel better too. It's the food and the lack of wandering around. Maybe even Tink's mindfulness session. At school, I have to count every other minute. Leashing the wolf like that is tiring. Here, I hang out in one of three rooms. Before coming here, I can't remember the last time I laughed out loud. I hope Peter's okay. I guess our illnesses don't really need much encouragement to go off the rails.

My illness.

Alone, in a rare moment in the rec room, I find a marker and draw a happy face on the ping-pong ball, using the dent for the mouth. Then I search out a book to read, curl up against the armrest of the couch and read until lights out. It almost feels normal.

In bed, I count to fall asleep. I tell myself it's not a new part of my ritual, but it's the second night in a row I've done it. It sort of makes sense, protecting the world one hundred percent before I shut down for the night, wrapping the world in it. And it works, so there's that. While I count I flex and relax each of my muscles like Tink talked about, and I don't remember finishing my count before drifting off.

Claws, fangs, yellow eyes fractured with veins greet me. But around the wolf's neck loops a collar of leather. While the wolf growls down, paws pressing into my hips, my mother looms above it, wrapping the leash about her hand and then wrist. Anger twists her face. Anger at what, I don't know, but she struggles. The wolf kicks backward and my mother's arms windmill as she tries for balance. The wolf breaks free. Jaws snap, and the snout tunnels into my armpit to haul out my book of tales. Loose pages drip from the binding.

"No!" my mother screeches.

No! I call and lunge after the relic. The wolf wants to destroy my magic. I begin to count, but the wolf only hunkers on the bed, placing the book between its paws and tearing at the pages. With each shake of its head, the spells are tatters.

My mother shoots at me the blackest of looks. Accusing me.

I wake. The threads of the dream unravel. My skin is wet, and I touch my face. Sweat runs in rivulets from my temples. I lean forward and pat the sheets until I feel the firm comfort of the solid hardback cover. But I can't shake my mother's glare. I *said* I was sorry, Mom.

Enough light from the park slips around the edges of the curtains for me to see. Sleeping Beauty's chest rises and falls. Red thrashes and moans from her bed. She is probably what woke me. Not that I mind. It's better than my dreams. I can see Pig's bed. It's empty.

I lie down and shut my eyes, starting to count to help myself fall back to sleep, but something draws me back. Pig's bed. Still empty. Something prickles along my spine. I don't know how long Pig's been gone, but it's already been too long for a bathroom trip. The last person who went missing tried to jump off the roof. I don't ever want to feel the sort of shame I do with Peter and, if Pig's leaving soon, maybe she's willing to do something drastic in order to stay. I swing my legs to the side of the bed and slide my feet into slippers.

The night nurse, I don't even know her name, looks up when I pad through the door, and I wave at her, pressing my legs together in the universal I-gotta-pee dance. She looks back down. The door off the unit is locked. The interview rooms are dark and empty. I count and peek into the rec room, which is deepest black and empty. That leaves the second patient room, 3B, the washroom and shower. I pad along the hall heading for the bathroom.

The shower's marked "In Use," but it's not on. I hear scuffling inside.

I pause with my hand on the doorknob. Maybe she's shy, having a late-night shower when no one's around to barge in. No one like me, right now. But maybe she's thrashing in a pool of blood. Maybe she is in there with wolves of her own making. I should get the nurse, and jog to the station.

. . . "Nurse," I whisper. "Pig's been in the shower a really long time."

She frowns. Her nametag reads: Jackie, and beside the name is a skeleton sticker. With a last look at a celebrity article, in which some A-list star probably got pregnant, or married, or divorced, or abducted by aliens, she swivels in her chair and meets me on my side of the hallway.

With a sharp rap of her knuckles on the door, Nurse Jackie says, "You okay in there?"

Someone swears and the scuffling intensifies. "Let me finish."

It's Vanet. I want to run. The nurse doesn't ask again; she throws open the door to reveal Vanet and Pig, both naked. Pig's flushed pink and has moved to the back of the room, but Vanet's standing there and turned toward the door, hanging free to the wind with his finger pointing at me.

"Really, Milly? Really?" he says and shakes his head.

"What do you think you're doing?" Nurse Jackie says. "Vanet—get your clothes and change in the hall. Eleanor, you need a swab before you get dressed. I'm phoning the on-call manager. Get yourselves back to bed, and I'll be filing a report."

"I don't want a swab," Pig says.

Nurse Jackie pauses as Pig pulls on her top. "That's fine, it's standard procedure, but instead Doctor Balder will be informed and you can have blood tests in the morning."

Vanet rolls his eyes, but Pig rushes past, bumping my shoulder as she does and enters 3A. Vanet doesn't bother putting anything on, bounces to his room, and slaps his ass as he crosses into it.

"You, too," Nurse Jackie says to me. "There will be extra security."

"Bitch," Pig says as I enter.

. . . "Sorry," I say. "I was worried about you."

"Don't. Ever. Worry. About. Me."

How could I be such an idiot? I must not have finished my count before falling asleep. Look what happened.

Chapter 18

"Group," Nurse Stenson calls after breakfast. Pig didn't even show to eat, but she is sitting in the rec room.

News of Pig and Vanet hooking up has spread to the other patients. I doubt it was Pig who told and it wasn't me, so I have to assume Vanet talked himself up. I'm not looking forward to this session.

Soon we're all seated in a haggard triangle with Pig as far away from Vanet as possible, and Vanet sitting as far as possible from me. Stenson ignores the geometrically challenged circle.

"Can anyone tell me the rules of group?" she asks.

Red rolls her eyes.

"Vanet, do you know the rules of group?" Stenson asks.

"Sure," he says.

"Is there one regarding relationships?"

"Report them." He snaps a salute.

"That's right, we have to understand the relationships of those within the unit. Is there a relationship you'd like to report?" He stares dumbly. "Anyone?"

"Why don't you ask Milly?" Pig says.

I try to shrink, but only manage to slip lower in my chair.

"Relationships like those of best friends and lovers are wonderful," Stenson says. "They change the way we see one another and that affects the group, so it is important that they be brought forward." Again, more silence. "No relationship? Nurse Jackie reports evidence of one last night. A relationship between Vanet and Eleanor."

"That?" Vanet laughs. "That wasn't a relationship. That was Pig unable to keep her hands off of me."

"What are you talking about?" Pig says to him. "You—" Then she clenches her hands into fists and shakes until her face pinks.

"Do you plan on continuing this relationship?" Stenson asks. Pig looks to Vanet.

"If she wants to meet me in the shower every once in a while, I'm in," he says with a shrug.

"I will remind everyone that sexual activities are not permitted on the ward," Stenson says to us all.

"So, no then, contraindicated," Vanet says. "What's the point, right?"

Pig shakes her dome. "Good."

Nurse Stenson clasps her hands as if that finishes the conversation. "Relationships are least of all about sex. Why do we need relationships? Wesley, why don't you start us off today?"

He sits staring at his hands for a minute until finally he says, "Supposed to help you, I guess."

"Very good," Stenson says with a little too much surprise in her tone. "Good relationships should benefit both parties. What's it called if only one party benefits? What might be happening?"

"Parenting," Red says and then flushes at Stenson's attention.

"Oh, good point," Stenson replies. "Parenting is a very close and important relationship in which both parent and child benefit from trust and love. How should a child benefit from a parent?"

"I was making a joke." Red starts her twitch.

"It's a good point, Red. There are different relationships like a friend to a friend, a parent to a child, or a child to a parent. These should all be positive, but in different ways."

"Yah," Vanet says. "Like I'm sure your dad's probably coming tomorrow with the keys to a new car. Total win."

Red seems to freeze, her eyes wide at first and then they shut tight. She shouts, "No!"

When she opens her eyes again, there's panic in them.

"What are you seeing, Red?" Stenson asks. "Is it the car crash? Are you seeing your mother?"

I don't know how long Red's been here. I think longer than everyone. She's searching the room, and when her eyes reach the exit, she jerks up. But Stenson opens her arms to her.

"No!" Red screams and then drops to her knees. "Mommy, no . . . ."

Stenson folds Red's head into her lap and then nods for us all to disappear.

After getting Pig and Vanet into trouble, I don't have many people I can talk to, so I follow Rottengoth to a corner of the rec room.

. . . "What's up with Red?" I whisper.

Red's still sobbing, but there's really nowhere else to go.

"PTSD," he says. "Post-traumatic stress disorder. A lot of us know one another from before. This is my third time through. Red relives a car accident she was in with her mom. Her mom died. Red survived. Happened months ago. She's been in and out of here ever since. Stenson keeps trying to bring it up, get her to see it as normal I think, but just talking about it really freaks Red out."

That makes sense. Seeing your mom cut out of a car would give anyone PTSD.

. . . "When are you going home?" I ask. "You seem a lot better." Part of me realizes that if Pig leaves and Red leaves, by next week I'll be the one explaining all of this to the new kids. I'll be the one newcomers look at sidelong and wonder if they belong with the likes of me.

Rottengoth shrugs. "I don't really care. At least here I don't have to deal with stuff."

. . . "I didn't mean to get Pig and Vanet in trouble," I say.

"I wouldn't worry about Vanet—Pig's mad, though."

Over in group, Red's calmed enough to sit back in the chair and talk quietly with the nurse. Pig glares at me over the top of a book that I know she's only pretending to read, because it's upside down. Peter's collecting coins with a game controller and I watch him, getting lost in the video-game fairy world of bright lights and sounds. It seems a bit hypocritical. They say Peter shouldn't be encouraged to dress up, but he's allowed to become a character in a game and play out his fantasy?

. . . "What's your fantasy?" I ask Rottengoth.

"What?" He's reading the *Lord of the Rings* trilogy.

. . . "What's your fantasy, not your dream, because I think dreams should be possible, your fantasy?"

"To obtain the *one ring to rule them all*," he says.

. . . "Come on."

"You first," he mumbles and turns the page.

. . . "I don't have one, that's why I'm asking."

"Nope. You first."

. . . "You know that short answers really suck for people who have to count. Anyway. I guess mine's to see my mom again. But if I can't have that . . . I want to kill the wolf."

"What wolf? You don't *have* to count, by the way. That's just a compulsion."

. . . "See, too short. Talk for a bit. I can count while you talk, and then by the time you're done I can speak, see? For the last three years I've been hunted by a wolf—wait." I hold a hand up. "I know it sounds crazy—but I've been holding it back with my count. It works like a magic spell, and it keeps others safe too, everyone. I've felt the wolf. I've seen it."

"Uh, huh. Balder calls them hallucinations. Nothing electroconvulsive therapy can't solve." To my eye roll he adds, "I just want to read. My short answers mean I have a hundred count to read. As for ECT, don't knock it till you've tried it. Works for me every time."

. . . "You're so annoying. I don't need shocks. If I kill the wolf, I won't need to count. I won't have OCD."

He lowers the book to stare over the top at me.

"Don't you get it? *That's* your wolf. Your OCD is your wolf. You don't need to kill anything, just need to see it for what it is and face it. Listen, man, we're all here because we're messed in the head. ECT and drugs, they're your shield against this wolf, but it's up to you to change the way you think about it."

It's my OCD. I hear it, and I hear it again. That OCD is something my brain has come up with to manage my anxiety. Staring at Rottengoth, seeing myself through his eyes, I get the tale about the chick who chose the pig farmer as her husband. I'm like the daughter who chose the huntsman and was never happy. It was all in her head. The pig farmer's wife took everything in stride and chose to be happy with what they had rather than unhappy with what they didn't have. That was her bow and arrows.

Rottengoth is back to reading.

I use the count to leave.

Nurse Jackie approaches with a smile, but her eyes are sad and glassy. "I was coming to find you. Doctor Balder wants to see you."

. . . "Where's Nurse Abby?" The smile on Jackie's face wanes.

"Nurse Abby is taking a short leave from work."

Oh. She's in trouble for what happened to Peter. For what I did. Jackie's having to take an extra shift. I try to remember if I counted properly yesterday and shake myself free of the urge.

It's your OCD.

A woman with a snake around her shoulders and a small cage is buzzed onto the unit.

That freaks me out.

I hurry toward interview room two, but the woman practically sprints to catch me, the snake's head bobbing.

I'm still counting when the white snake flicks its pink tongue at me.

"My name's Adelia, and these are my pets. I've never met you before. Would you like to pat Slither or hold Scabbers the rat?"

She lifts the cage hanging from her forearm. Whiskers poke out of slots. "Snakes and rats are hypoallergenic." I shake my head at Slither's cold eyes. "Well, let me know, but you'll have to wait your turn for Scabbers. Red has a special connection with him."

I hop into the interview room and sit.

As I wait, I listen to her go from room to room, asking if anyone wants to hold her creatures—some kind of pet therapy. Balder's on doctor-schedule and arrives ten minutes later. By that time, I've decided not to tell him about the wolf. If I kill the OCD, I kill the wolf. If what Rottengoth says is correct, Balder will see it as hallucinations and will put me on more drugs, or shock me, and that will keep me from the dance for sure.

"Sorry," the doctor says and flips up the chart as he shuts the interview room door. "Romila—Milly, okay, so you've had a few days now and I understand from Nurse Stenson that you've been an active participant in group activities. Which is good, because we won't let you leave otherwise." He laughs at that as if it's a shared joke. "I'm going to ramble on for a bit given the OCD counting ritual. I'll be removing Todd. Not that you're eating as much as we'd like, but I don't see any significant evidence of an eating disorder that isn't related to your OCD. Control the OCD and you'll eat well. We are going to continue the liquid meal supplement with your diet. Any questions so far?"

I blink at him. His lips twitch at the sight of my counting.

. . . "Yay to no more Toadie, and I told you I didn't have an eating disorder. I do have a question. Can I go to the dance?"

He waits for long enough to ensure he's not interrupting and then replies. "It's not polite to call Todd names. As for the dance, we'll have a family meeting tomorrow morning, and we'll make a decision then, that seem fair? No more fainting? You're okay with what happened with Pig and Vanet?"

I shake my head.

. . . "A meeting with my stepmom isn't a *family* meeting."

"Point taken. But I think it's time to challenge your OCD. Let's set a goal. A small goal. How would you like to get rid of that hop of yours?"

I nod, but even thinking about it sends a wave of anxiety crashing over me. My cheeks heat while my stomach roils. This is it. This is what Rottengoth talked to me about. Facing the wolf head-on. Then why do I feel naked and hollow?

The doctor claps his hands. "Great! What I want you to do is stand next to the door and complete your count so that you're ready. When you're done, I'll count to three, and I want you to crawl through the door. You can't hop while on your hands and knees, so crawl."

Out of all my compulsions, the hop is one I see as a bit silly. I mean, I've already counted so, whether real or not, the wolf is held back. The hop is like punctuation.

I slowly kneel and place my hands near the threshold.

"Well done," Balder says. "I want you to rate your anxiety level. Ideally I'd love to hear your thoughts, but under the circumstances . . . maybe you can use your fingers. With ten being I can't take this anymore and one being no anxiety at all."

On my hands and knees, I lean out over the threshold and hold up seven fingers. *Hop or die.* I cringe. *Shut up, OCD—hop and look like an idiot.* I swear it's like someone has clamped their hands around my throat.

"Your OCD can't hurt you," Balder says. "It's your mind

telling your body to react."

Still, this doesn't feel right. Eight fingers. I'm not ready. How can I use a weapon that's fighting me? The hero hasn't completed her training.

I place a hand on the other side of the threshold—but pull it back as if it's burned. Nine fingers. The wolf's swinging back, crashing through trees. The Dark Wood presses into the room. I've waited too long now and have to count again. Balder seems to get it.

"It's okay. This time try both hands and if that's okay, a knee. You will feel anxious about it, but it can't hurt you."

He's not the one unable to breathe. Eight fingers. Eight. *I can tell you no more.*

This time I manage the two hands, but when I slide my knee up, I retch. Ten fingers—at least, I'd show him ten fingers if I wasn't so busy trying to hold in barf with them. Does it matter if the wolf's not real? Isn't my OCD just as bad?

"Great work," Balder says, and I don't know what he's talking about, because I almost threw up and then died. I had no idea I was so sick. Tears well in my eyes and I struggle to hide them. "Let me get back to the roots of your OCD."

We both sit back down. I draw deep breaths, my OCD reminding me with the renewed threat of retching this isn't over yet.

"Tell me about when you first started counting. The first time you recall the urge."

A sense of danger sweeps through my bones. . . . "I'd had some rituals before. Kid stuff. Using the same cup. Always putting on my shoes the same way. But it really got going after my mom became sick. I'd do the cooking, and I'd check the oven ten times to make sure the oven was off, and I worried that our dog had crawled into it and would be baking like the kids in Hansel and Gretel.

"I measured everything to make sure the recipes were okay, and I wasn't giving everyone diabetes or poisoning them, but still, I'd ask if they felt okay after. But everyone makes mistakes, right?" I shake my head. "When my dad met Adriana, she cooked, and at first it was a big relief, but then other things didn't feel right. The OCD changed to counting. As long as I do the count, it feels safer, more right, and I'm allowed to speak or move and it will be okay, nothing will attack me. I also wondered if my stepmom was trying to kill me or my dad. So I wouldn't eat."

I can tell by the interest on Balder's face that he really thinks we're getting somewhere and hope blooms warm in my gut.

"So you remember a time when you didn't count, but had other compulsions?"

I nod. And it's true. The wolf hasn't always been there.

"This won't be easy," he says. "It's work. Hard work, but I know you can do it. Milly, I'm going to start you on a low dose of an antidepressant."

Am I always going to need drugs now?

"Do you understand that your counting is a compulsion to count, not actually saving the world? That's why compulsions can change. It's your OCD and OCD is manageable."

I'm not buying it.

"I want you to work on tab yellow in *Rock-on*. And there's someone I'd like you to meet tomorrow," Balder continues. "He's in an acute room and I think he'd like some company and you'd both benefit from the experience."

145

I'm counting as fast as I possibly can.

. . . "I don't think that's a good idea," I say, holding up nine fingers.

"Why not, Milly? What are you afraid of?"

There are some doors you simply don't open. Doors that hold wolves.

. . . "Isn't he a total zombie?"

"Nope, his treatment is progressing well. Wolfgang's here for help with OCD just like you."

Just like you. Wolfman is just like me?

"And he's grown much stronger."

That I can believe.

Chapter 19

I count very carefully as I cross the thresholds back to my room. I'm stunned that I will meet the wolf tomorrow. Face-to-face.

He's grown much stronger.

I want to talk to Bill but he won't be home yet, so I start on homework as a distraction. Red twitches at her desk beside me. She's patting Scabbers the rat. Pig lies in her bed staring at the ceiling.

. . . "Sorry about your mom," I say to Red.

Her head snaps around. "Don't talk about her." And then she goes back to twitching and patting the rat.

. . . "Maybe your dad—"

She screeches, covering her ears with her palms.

I hold up my hands in surrender and doodle on a biology assignment. Stenson comes in and replaces Sleeping Beauty's IV bag, and the girl sleeps on. Healing with or without Jesus, while Toadie sits by her bed.

I count for her. I guess it's a form of prayer. My family has never been big into religion; I wonder if I'd be a counter if I had a god to talk to. To pray to keep the devil back. Imagine if I swapped Hail Mary's for counts! A hundred Hail Mary's? I'd never get anything done.

The title to the yellow tab reads *Freak Out Here.*

Everyone freaks out a bit, but you do it a lot. Get a grip on it here. Write down anytime you think things like:

What if some dude sees me flip out? Or, what if I botch it? Or, what if they think I'm candy-ass and hassle me?

Put those in column one. In the second column write down something that runs against those dumbass thoughts. Who cares, man?! So they hassle me, then what?

But dude, you're messed, right? So your head keeps jamming and says if that happens, then kaboom, right? Total meltdown. They'll think I'm wiggin' out! They'll beat me up. They'll say I suck.

Put all that stuff in column three and then write what you really think about all that crap in the fourth column. Who cares what they think? What are the chances that they'll actually throw a punch—not high, dude! I don't suck, they suck.

But you're thinking, what if it does *happen, right? They start beating on you. What would you do? Write that in column five. I'd go to the heat and finger the badasses, but you come up with your own gnarly ideas.*

At the bottom of the page is written: *Get in the zone!*

This is messed. But I like it. I have these thoughts all the time—minus the sixties slang. Like, every other minute I have thoughts like these. They're so automatic I'm not even sure I thought of them as thoughts, more like truths. Things so obvious I didn't really need to pick them apart. *Of course there will be doors at the mall, so I shouldn't bother going. Even if I do count right, I'd slow down my friends. People would make fun of me. They might leave me behind and then I'd be alone and someone could murder me.* Yeah, stuff like that. All because of—doors. Doors lead to death. The Dark Wood.

I set to it and for half an hour fill the page in before I run out of things to say. The snake woman knocks and enters the room. Red has nearly petted the fur off the rat.

The pet person plucks the rat up by its tail and the snake around her neck becomes *very* alert. "What a good boy," she says.

Red nods to her desk and wrings her empty hands.

. . . "I've never heard of therapy rats and snakes," I say.

"I know," the woman says, "so misunderstood, some of the most loving and cuddly creatures on Earth. Besides, rats are cheap and some of my patients have trouble with how much love they show. This here's Scabbers the Fourth. Do you want to hold Slither? I'm on my way out, but I can stay a moment."

Slither's jaws are open and the head is slowly moving toward the upside-down rat.

. . . "Slither's looking a little too cuddly, I'll pass," I say.

The woman swats the snake's head without even looking and it pulls back. She shrugs and slips the rat into his carrier as she leaves. The IV bag must be empty too, because Stenson pops in, unhooks the IV and follows Toadie out.

When they're gone, I summon the courage to talk to Pig. . . . "Can I ask you a question, Pig?" I wince, ready for her to snap.

"You're talking to me?" she says. "Seriously?"

. . . "I'm really sorry. I didn't know you guys were a thing. I didn't mean to cause a problem."

"We're not. Just sex." She flips over and buries her face in her pillow.

I go back to doodling, but after a minute she groans and flips back over. "What did you want?"

In here you can't afford to not talk to people. . . . "What do you know about Wolfgang? Why's he here?"

Pig squints at me.

"I heard he's a bit like you. Not a counter but all serious OCD, so many compulsions he didn't even move at first. But he used to move. A killer. Got caught, because of OCD. He had to be clean, right? Had these elaborate rituals that took hours to complete. Eventually it was like he caught himself."

. . . "You're full of crap and that's not like me," I say.

Pig shrugs. "More than you might think."

. . . "Then who did he kill?" I ask, folding my arms.

"Who?" Pig asks. "What's the plural of who, because they're still tracking down the full body count."

I shudder even though I know her ridiculous stories shouldn't bother me. Red's shoulders are jerking up and down again.

"I'm meeting Wolfgang tomorrow," I say. "Supposed to help me with my treatment."

Pig laughs. "Sounds to me like someone wants to get rid of you."

I try to lose myself in homework, but I keep glancing at the black square on the desk that had once held the wolf.

When it's four, I rush to the phone and call Billy.

"Hello?" he asks.

I tap the handset three times.

"Oh, hey, Milly, how're you doing? I heard that you're not in the hospital. The psych ward? Because of your counting. I understand why you didn't say anything. What's it like there?

Do people jabber on at you about aliens and stuff? Are you on drugs? Have you had shock therapy? If you're on drugs, try to save a few so I can try it too."

. . . "Who said?" I ask, and I'm so stunned I pause too long.

"Um . . . everyone just knows."

Everyone knows. No one will ever be my friend again.

. . . "Whatever. Yes, I'm in the psychiatric unit, but it's still the hospital. I have an anxiety disorder and I'm not taking anything for it yet. No shocks either, but you'd be amazed how well that works. People here may be a bit weird, but pretty cool too."

"Really? I hear they've tried to kill themselves or run around naked and stuff. Didn't some fairy kid try to fly? It was on the news."

My fingers whiten as they grip the phone. I bet it's Adriana feeding everyone gossip.

. . . "That fairy kid is intellectually disabled and is actually really nice, and sure people have been naked, and they do help people here who try to commit suicide or are thinking about that, but that's better than having it happen, right? Listen, *I'm* one of these people."

There's silence on the other end of the line and my voice echoes in the hallway.

"Whoa, you're not thinking about suicide, are you?"

I stare at the phone. . . . "No, I'm just saying. It's not as rare as everyone thinks and it's nothing to make fun of. It's an illness like cancer. You wouldn't tease someone for having cancer, would you?"

"Chill . . . Okay, well, sorry."

I have to turn this conversation around.

. . . "I'm looking forward to the dance," I say, lightening my tone. "I miss you. Everyone."

There's a pause. "About the dance. Are you sure you're okay? . . . To come back. Everyone's going to be there, you might want to ease back into school or something. The dance will be insane."

Insane.

I inspect the handset again, my throat tightening, my eyes watering. . . . "Yes, I'm fine. Are you going to be fine? For me to come back. Everyone's going to be there. You sure you want to be seen with me? I *could* be insane."

"I didn't mean it like that."

. . . "I know. I'm sorry. I *am* worried what people will think, but I don't think there's a good way to go back. Maybe it's like ripping off a Band-Aid. Better for everyone to see me at once."

"Yeah. Okay, then. But I'm not sure I want to go anyway."

. . . "Oh." My voice cracks.

"It's just—"

I hang up.

The conversation leaves me cold. He's embarrassed. Worse. He doesn't want to be seen with me. I know it. And me having to call him means I can't determine if he's still into me based on if he calls me back. This sucks. I have to escape before it ruins my life.

I count to a hundred and hop through the door to dinner. Why would Billy be embarrassed? We'll just hop and count everywhere, right? I'm such a loser. I'll never stop counting, so why do I bother?

No. I can do this.

Pig's found a new table, but Vanet and Red are still at mine. Red's a wreck. She's shaking. Sweat beads on her forehead. Her skin is waxen. If her father really is coming tomorrow, I hope it cheers her up.

Today's hospital dinner lives up to every cliché. It's leathery pressed beef of some sort, mushy broccoli, pasta with a runny red sauce and coconut pudding. I hate coconut. I don't even know why coconut's a flavor option. Why coconut and not strawberry? Or cherry? Or lemon? I bet the hospital bought it at a discount.

"No more Toadie!" Pig exclaims after I sit down. She pushes back from the chair and shrugs an apology at Rottengoth and Peter, whom she's ditching. When she slides her platter next to mine, she says, "If you really want to show you're sorry, you'll give me your dessert."

Total win-win. I purse my lips as if this is hurting me and place the pudding on her platter.

"Two days to go and I can finally get good eats," Pig says. "You still need some better kinda punishment, though. Teach you a lesson, isn't that right, Vanet?"

Vanet laughs. "Too bad we don't have a guillotine. Banned them a decade ago from all psych wards."

I'm not sure I want any punishment a guy like Vanet can cook up.

I don't eat a lot, but I eat steadily, the mystery-meat waning to a half moon, the soggy broccoli disappearing entirely. At the end, Stenson drops a pill in my hand.

"Wait," Vanet says. "Don't show us the pill." He points to Red, who sighs.

"Prozac," she guesses.

"I dunno, aspirin," Pig says. "No, Paxil."

"Zoloft," Vanet completes the circle.

"None of your business," Stenson says.

I open my palm to show everyone.

"Prozac. Red wins," Vanet says. "I'll give you five bucks for it."

"May cause dizziness, drowsiness, trouble sleeping, sweating, rashes, vomiting, anxiety, diarrhea . . . miss anything?" Pig asks.

"Death," Vanet says.

I stare at the green and white pill.

I pop it in my mouth and dry swallow.

. . . "All better," I say.

We clear our platters and I start my count to leave. I hear whispers behind me, but I remind myself that I'm on the psych ward. When I pause at the door, Vanet shouts, "Now!"

I'm being punished. Hands shove me over the threshold.

I'm only at sixty-two.

Chapter 20

I land on my knees. They burn against the cold linoleum. The rush of blood into my head muffles Pig and Vanet's laughter, pounding my eardrums. My chest tightens. Heat rolls through me and boils into my knotted stomach. My heart rams against my ribs but not steadily, more like a sprint in which I keep running faster, tripping like the girl in bad horror movies, stumbling over roots and running farther and farther into the Dark Wood while the wolf gains on her no matter how fast and desperately she scrambles.

"What's wrong with me?" I call out without counting. I clamber to my feet, stretch my neck out to the ceiling, but I can't find enough air. The hallway walls pulse. I pace toward the exit, but it's locked, and I hurry back toward the rec room.

"Take it easy," Vanet says as I pass him. "It was just a joke."

My vision shimmers. I start running but I'm not counting and veer from the open doorway at the last second, my shoulder striking the wall. I turn to press my back against the plaster and then run back, each breath searing. Stenson grabs my arm at the nursing station.

"It's okay," she says, but it's not. "Walk it off. Walk it off."

I slow a bit, but more in utter confusion. Jackie has cleared the hall for me, but the other kids watch from doorways. I hold my hands to my eyes like a cart horse's blinkers.

My heart will explode. It has to. I'm going to die.

The vomit heaves out of me so quickly I don't have time to ask for a bucket, or to count into the washroom. I'm bent over and it splatters all over the floor. In the midst of the meat and pasta and broccoli lies my little magic pill. The one that causes death.

My head balloons and I imagine it's as big as the hall with more blood rushing to it. It'll split. Pop like a squashed melon to spatter walls and ceiling. A messy, embarrassing death.

I can't breathe. I suck back in and choke on the barf. Darkness closes in on me. I can sense the Dark Wood looming at my back. Wolfgang. The leader of the pack. I scream.

I'm going to die; it's just a question of how. Heart attack, choking, or slobbering jaws.

"Shh . . . It's okay. You're having a panic attack, honey," Stenson says. "It's okay. Everything will be fine in a few minutes."

I don't have a few minutes. How can she say that? There's a hundred percent chance something terrible is happening. My spell's broken. Maybe it'll be my dad who suffers. Maybe I'll cause the death of Adriana. I never wanted her dead. I have to call her. This has happened before. It has. I've shut it out for so long, but I've counted before and the spell worked—I made my wishes real. I remember.

The first time I counted: I hadn't told Doctor Balder the truth about it. I remember it so clearly now. I rushed home from school. From playing basketball, even with all those court lines. I hadn't stopped at doorways or checked my locker lock to ensure it was snapped shut. I'd biked home and rushed inside to hand my mom my report card.

Like usual she was all tense and pale. Dinner steamed on the table. She'd even turned the napkins into swans, but I swear I only wanted a sandwich and to go and see my friends. I told her so as I handed her my report card. It was a good one. As and Bs, one B- in geography, but only because I can't draw well and the teacher seemed to love diagrams.

She shook her head at the report card and told me that it certainly left room for improvement, and that she didn't feel well and to eat whatever I damn well pleased. She didn't care anymore. She only wished I could appreciate her.

It came to a head. All her hovering over me, her constant drive for perfection, that I could never be good enough.

I counted after that. It was like casting a spell. I hadn't counted so that she'd be okay, or that I'd be okay, or so we could fix whatever was wrong between us. I'd counted so that she'd leave. A week later she was diagnosed with cancer. My counting had killed her. No amount of counting reversed it.

I made her die.

. . . "Adriana," I croak.

"Shh . . . We'll call her right away," Stenson says. But maybe it's the wolf wanting me to call. It would want her to come here, to die on the way. My fault. Again.

I shake my head.

. . . "No car," I say. "Don't let her drive. Or walk. Stay in the house. Lock up."

But I can do something. I have magic of my own. I start to count again. This time I count for her. To ensure she's safe.

I'm going to die. I'm going to die.

"You're not going to die, Milly," Stenson says and since she can't read my mind, I must be saying it and not counting. My stomach pumps in and out with the shallow and ridiculous breaths. I have to count.

Slowly, slowly, the sense of dread dissipates. And I realize that the terrible thing did happen. It happened to me. The terrible thing was the attack. Nurse Jackie hands Stenson a warm cloth and she wipes my forehead, cheeks, and then mouth.

Supported at each elbow, they walk me to my room, where I dig in my heels at the threshold.

. . . And then we're through. I'm so tired. It's like I've run a million miles, and maybe my heart did. Maybe I've used up ten years of my life. My brain is almost sixteen, but my heart is twenty-six. The dread surges again, but I lack the strength for it to take hold. My limbs sink into the bed and continue down. It's like Tink's relaxation exercise, but I can't stop it this time. Belatedly I remember to count, the shot of adrenaline giving me a final chance before I succumb to fatigue.

But there's no oblivion. Only the wolf.

It spends no time clawing beneath the bedroom door, simply slipping through the bottom like a slick of oil. It reforms and sprints across the floor. But as it launches into the air, my mother tackles it and pulls a length of chain from her back. Growling and snarling fills the air as she works to restrain the beast. Triumphant, my mother smiles over it squirming on the floor. It begins to yowl, a mournful sound that causes me to sit up and swing my legs off the bed.

My mother's eyes are hard and proud. Seeing me, the wolf seems to give up and lies with its snout upon great paws.

"I'm sorry, Mom," I say. "I'm so sorry."

My mother turns to me, "Are you?"

Why, even knowing what I've done, does she make me so angry? Guilt presses like a boulder on my chest. She only ever wanted the best for me. Only ever protected me and urged me to be better. Like she protects me now, from the wolf.

"But . . . ." But there's nothing to say because, at my mother's words, the wolf gathers all of its strength and bursts from my mother's chains, pounding its paws into her chest and then, the huge gray barrel-head swivels left and it launches on Pig, savaging her throat. Pig screams. I scream.

I wake to Adriana running her fingers through my hair. I turn into them, but the band of her gold watch scratches along my cheek. I rear back.

"Milly," she says.

. . . "Wolf," I say.

Her lips thin. Still, she asks, "Are you okay? The nurse tells me you had a panic attack after you were pushed through a doorway."

I nod. My hand rests on the cover of my book.

"You hadn't counted. I came as soon as I could."

I nod again. I begin to wonder if that's true or whether she was having a manicure and finished it before driving over, taking a scenic route. But my eyelids are already on their way back down.

Adriana licks her lips and opens her mouth as if she has something to say, but isn't quite sure how to put it. "Know how

I like everything just so. Perfect? Always on time and neat?" she asks, and it's like her to start talking about herself when I'm the one in need of help.

. . . "Yeah," I say.

"Well . . . I've had panic attacks before, too." My eyes flutter. "Panic attacks feel as though the world is trying to crush you. So scary. I'm so sorry."

. . . "We're a real pair," I whisper and shut my eyes for good.

"Hello, Doctor Balder," Adriana says. I can sense his looming presence. He has an aura about him, a dark aura. I hear the word—*setback*.

"She's awake?" he asks.

"Fading," she replies.

. . . "Hi, Doctor," I say. "I'm okay." I keep my eyes closed, though, as if opening them would tap me of any remaining energy.

"It's entirely normal for Milly to be exhausted after a panic attack," he says.

There it is again. Panic attack. It makes it sound as though it's all in my head. It wasn't. I miscounted and I almost died.

"This has never happened before," Adriana says. "Sure, she's been anxious, but never to the point of collapse."

"It's part of the spectrum of an anxiety disorder, triggered by being shoved through a door. It's not surprising. It is, however, treatable."

"What will happen to the other patients?" she asks. "That was an assault."

"Why don't we wait for Milly to sleep on it and let her talk about whether any punishment is warranted?"

"I can press charges." It's the first time I've heard Adriana with her hackles up like this, and my eyes flick open.

"How do you feel, Milly?" Doctor Balder asks.

... "Just tired," I say and he nods. "I don't want to press charges." I nearly killed Peter. I embarrassed Vanet and Pig, or at least Pig. I'd call it even.

"We can talk about that later," he says.

"Doctor Balder tells me you've been asking to go to the dance tomorrow," Adriana says. "I don't think you should be going to the dance."

"We can discuss that tomorrow, too," Doctor Balder says, and in a way that implies visiting hours are over.

My eyes flutter back down. Although I hate Adriana for saying it, I don't want to go to the dance anymore. Imagine if I have a panic attack there? No, I don't even want to leave the hospital, let alone return to school.

I'm fading. Fade to black.

Chapter 21

Red paces the hall. It's Friday. Halloween. Her father's coming to see her. He wants to discuss her returning home. I watch through our room's open door. Every ten seconds she streaks past. Like clockwork. Six Reds is one minute. Sixty Reds is ten minutes. He's not due for another three hundred and sixty Reds. Both of us have been excused from group, but I wonder if she could use the distraction. They're reviewing progress to goals. I would have nothing to say about any of that. I never again want to feel the way I felt last night. Like I was bursting into flame.

I bury my head in the book of tales. If the wolf came after the book, then maybe the answer to the wolf's final destruction lies within the pages.

Breakfast was a non-starter. I've had a *setback*. Even now nausea builds and subsides in me like ocean waves, the crest rising with my bile and the trough leaving me sucked low and empty of energy. When Stenson handed me my pill this morning, her cheeks seemed hollow, eyes too bright—witchy. She wore a pointed black hat. I shuddered but kept quiet. Wolves, witches, Pig, Red, fairies, Sleeping Beauty, I need little more evidence of where I am. Where this is headed. I am in some sort of fairy tale world, a different plane of existence maybe. If I need to peel back the fairy tale to get better, then maybe the same fairy tale has the power to bury me for trying. We all know how those fairy tales really ended, don't we? No huntsman saved Little Red Riding Hood. The wolf ate her and that was that.

Red streaks past and I doze off watching for her to pass again. I wake to the now familiar click and buzz of the ward door opening. The weight of my book is a comfort. Red rocks on her bed. The poor girl watched her mother being cut out of the car wreck. What would that do to someone like me? Having to relive it in my mind like she does. Spontaneous combustion. Baked like that witch tried to do to Hansel and Gretel. Their stepmother hadn't wanted them either.

Nurse Stenson steps to the door. Her lips are drawn back as if perpetually smiling. Her twisted teeth glint in the institutional lighting. A glow touches her cheeks. I've never heard of a witch blushing.

"Your father's waiting," Stenson says to Red.

Red nods to herself, rubs her legs and hops up. She meets him at the bedroom door.

Her father has the sort of square jaw that women seem to like. A cashmere sweater with a neat V-neck stretches at his shoulders. His Adam's apple juts; his body moves with lean muscle, and his smile is bright and welcoming.

"Honey," he says and enfolds Red in his arms. Red stiffens in the hug, but he rubs his hand up and down her spine. Up and down. Up. And. Down. "I missed you."

He steps back a little and, gripping her shoulders, stares at her with clear blue eyes. "You look better," he says, but she doesn't; she looks like a wreck. Even I can tell she's lost weight and hasn't slept since I arrived, not unless you call a constant nightmare sleep. "Which interview room would you like, one or two?"

As if that's even a choice.

"Here," she says. "Can we stay here?" She shifts so that she's leaning back into our room.

"That's not fair to the other patients who need their rest," he says. "One or two." She goes to speak again and he cuts her off. "One or two. I'd like to talk to you in private."

And then she's gone, sucked through the door into one or two. Something's wrong here. I feel it in my marrow, but nausea crests into my throat. I cough spittle into a bucket at my side.

Laughter erupts from group in the rec room, and I wonder what they're cackling about. I must have appeared crazed last night. I wonder if Pig's angry because I didn't show to breakfast so she couldn't eat my leftovers. Sleeping Beauty draws deep breaths. Maybe it's me, but her breathing seems easier than it has been, but that's probably because they backed off her chemo.

A knock comes at the door.

"Milly, do you feel up to meeting Wolfgang?" Doctor Balder asks, now in full wizard regalia. A blue, sparkly hat boasts matching stars with those on his coat, which is cinched with a blue silk sash.

"Wolfgang's OCD also gets him to do a number of things, and I think it would help if you both shared your experiences with one another."

. . . "What about the panic attack?" I ask. My hands begin to wring each other out. "Will it happen again?"

"Well, I suspect this isn't your first episode, Milly. Do you recall what you told me about the day you fainted in gym class?" I shake my head. "The day you fainted, you said you were anxious about having to navigate doors and lines on the gym floor."

He's right.

. . . "I had a panic attack, didn't I? Oh my god, what am I going to do?"

"Losing consciousness during an attack is very uncommon and I think your lack of nutrition played a role. I also think when you first arrived here, you had something of a panic attack."

. . . "Then what about last night? I'm eating well, and I almost died!"

He presses his lips together before responding. "I am of two minds on that. One is that the attack was due to a very powerful trigger. A trigger we'll try to ensure doesn't happen again. Secondly, you should put it into perspective. Panic attacks are really common in anxiety disorders. What you need to know about them is that despite how they may feel, they will not hurt you and they will pass within a few minutes. I assure you that you did not almost die, even if you felt that way."

The certainty in his voice makes me wish I believed him. . . . "Okay," I say, but I'm quaking. I don't want to continue this treatment if I have to feel this way every day. It's time to face the wolf, but I also know what I am to him. I'm the lame deer at the back of the herd. Diseased, weakened, young, and easy prey.

I hop through the door, and flush for still having to hop. I follow Doctor Balder down the hall where he opens the door to the acute room and steps through.

"Wolfgang," he says. "This is the girl I was telling you about: Milly."

"Where is she?" The voice is brittle and under tight control. "Doesn't she know how little time I have left?" he asks.

"We've found nothing wrong with you," Doctor Balder says. "You've many decades left. More than enough time for Milly to talk to you."

Having finished my count, I step to the threshold of the room but don't enter. I was counting to speak.

"Hi." I'm about to say more and am left staring and glad I hadn't hopped inside. Wolfgang's room is white and he is white. Well, not his skin. That's dark brown and burnished in places to a painful-looking red, but he's draped in a white poncho and wearing white shoes. He's no longer unshaven, and his eyes, far from being dead, now twitch with life. A white turban still wraps his head.

"I'm filthy," he says.

He's not what I expected.

... "Let me guess, you think you're dying and are compulsively clean," I say and it sounds rude, but it's not meant to be, we both know why we're here. For me, though, what's more important is that Pig was lying. Wolfgang's as much of a wolf as I am. This isn't the wolf. Not the one from my nightmares. And it's a new ring to clutch. If my fears were unfounded here, then maybe none of them are real.

Wolfgang touches his neck.

"You're a counter, that it?" he asks. "Count before you speak?"

And we start talking, and as we do, I understand why Balder

brought me here. We trade our obsessions like two kids trading hockey cards.

"I touch my neck a lot, I feel things crawling there." Wolfgang holds his hand away and then it starts to shake before he itches at a particularly red spot, the relief obvious.

. . . "Don't worry," I say. "I have this hop that I do when I go through doors."

He smiles at that. "You actually hop? Like a bunny or a kangaroo?"

Outside the door I do a little jump to show him, and he laughs.

"Okay, so the one I get teased about the most is round objects," he says. "They terrify me."

I stare at him, confused.

"Balls. Oranges. Wheels," he explains.

. . . "Whoa—that's pretty random. But it's just your OCD, right? All in your head." I can say this because the counting might seem just as stupid to him, something I do in order to manage my anxiety instead of facing the anxiety itself. If I'd waited longer before getting treatment, I might have grown as bad as Wolfgang—frozen by anxiety.

"So they tell me."

. . . "I've started counting to go to sleep and count a sort of prayer to each person in my life, so that they'll stay safe too."

"Sounds to me like a good reason not to get to know too many people. I don't like the sort that tries to touch me."

What's weird is that I understand what he's saying about touching—he's worried about germs—but my first impression was that he's talking about abuse. And with that thought, I suddenly know what's happening with Red. I suspect why no one's figured out how to help her. Her PTSD isn't about her car accident at all.

In the ten minutes I've been here, standing on the opposite side of the door as if Wolfgang's in a clean room, he's checked his pulse eighteen times.

"What do you think of Wolfgang's compulsions?" Doctor Balder asks me.

. . . "Pretty crazy." I chuckle. "I don't see how round objects can hurt anyone and he's not dying."

"Do you think Wolfgang's obsessions are a part of him or are they a part of his OCD?"

. . . "Well, OCD, right?"

"It's not a test, Milly. But I agree with you. His obsessions are just that, something to be dealt with. Nothing to be anxious about, just exposed for what they are. He's not dying, nor are you causing anyone else to die when you don't count."

I nod. No wolf.

. . . "But . . . how do you fight it?"

"When Wolfgang first arrived, he was paralyzed by his compulsions into total inaction. He's had ECT, combined with drugs and now psychotherapy. After his medications took effect, he improved rapidly but has a long way to go. Now he's doing what you're doing. Exposing himself to his compulsions with the goal of reducing anxiety."

"You're part of my therapy," Wolfgang says. "Your breath has a lot of germs. And you carry a lot of disease."

. . . "Not to mention my round head," I say with a smile, which he returns.

"Thank you, Wolfgang," Doctor Balder says, and Wolfgang runs to his sink where he dips a brush into the tap water and begins scrubbing his forearms raw.

"Green tab, Milly, for our next meeting," Balder says and signals that he'll be staying with Wolfgang.

The door closes in my face with a click.

At the end of the hall, Red's being hugged goodbye by her father. He's crying, saying how much he misses her and that he'll see her soon. She's crying too, but I'm pretty sure it's for very different reasons. Some wolves are all too real.

Chapter 22

On the thought board, I write: *Who's your wolf?*

Milly: ???
Wesley: Parents
Pig: Mother
Peter: Fairies/Witch
Vanet: ??
Red: Father

It's afternoon, before group. I left lunch early, compelled to write this on the thought board. Maybe someone knows who my secret wolf is. But what's important is that I know Red's.

Her PTSD isn't just the car crash. It's also about her father. A father who wants to take her home this evening.

A few other notes are on the board. *I'm going to miss Red.* And: *In the land of the crazies, we are all sane.* Vanet wrote that last bit. It goes without saying that the inverse is true.

Stenson's taking group today, and I'm happy about that. Tink couldn't handle me as the hunter. I can change Red's story if I can arrive before her wolf. Rottengoth wanders in first. I wonder why he's still here. Well, I know he was depressed, but he seems okay. But here is the land of crazies. It's weird that we feel better amongst other sick people. It's a strange little community. And the thought reminds me how far I've come. That I realize I'm sick. Maybe that means I can get better.

I've always known my counting didn't make sense, not really, but it's easier than dealing with the anxiety and it wasn't a problem, because everyone adapted their lives around me. I have to start working through it. Today, I will stop the hop. If that works, maybe I'll try counting by twos or fives or even tens.

The wood looms darkly. One step at a time.

I sit in a chair. Pig walks into the rec room, rubbing her stomach. She's been almost as twitchy as Red as of late, but she's always more relaxed with a full belly. At lunch, I chugged the can of Ensure they gave me and then let Pig go to town on my sandwich.

Vanet's next, followed by Peter, as bouncy and happy as ever. Red arrives, scratching her arms like a crack addict. Stenson drags Rottengoth into the room, pauses when she reads what's written on the thought board, and then sits.

"Welcome to group, everyone." She smiles, carrying a small plastic pumpkin with candies. "Today is a special day where one of us moves on. I'd like that to be our theme this afternoon. The unit offers support from staff and patients, but outside we need to depend on others and ourselves. How can we cope with challenges after we leave?" She holds up a tiny Mars bar as a reward.

I'm disappointed. I want to talk about wolves.

. . . "How do you know you're ready?" I ask. "I mean, Red doesn't look ready. Are you ready?"

Stenson holds up her hand to Red. "That's a very complex discussion, Milly, and is really one best had between doctor, guardian, and patient. There's always a lot of work to be done after you leave. For everyone."

This isn't good enough. I need an axe to cut Red out of her wolf.

Forty-two . . .

"How can we cope outside of the hospital?" Stenson asks again.

"Think happy thoughts," Vanet replies, and everyone but Red and me giggles.

"We can try to stay positive, yes, I think that's very important," Stenson says, tossing him the chocolate bar. "Wesley?"

"I can take my meds. Find better parents, I guess." Rottengoth sounds doubtful, but a Kit-Kat lands in his lap.

"Great, it is important that we stay on our medications and continue the exercises Doctor Balder has prescribed."

"Can I give group a miss?" Red blurts. "I'm leaving and everything."

Stenson shakes her head. "All the more reason for you to stay."

. . . "What do you mean, find better parents, Wes?" I ask.

He flushes and his head hangs impossibly lower. "I dunno. I don't think social services will find anyone."

"There are some wonderful group homes," Stenson says.

Pig laughs at that. "Sure, if you like brothers who'll steal your stuff and house mothers who just want you to stay quiet."

. . . "I don't understand, aren't you going home to your parents?" I ask.

Red's legs gallop. "Group is like picking at scabs."

"My parents are separated and neither wants custody of me," Rottengoth says. "They are fighting over who gets my brother, but neither will take me. That's why I'm still here."

. . . "Oh, sorry," I say.

Stenson brings our attention back: "I see that someone has written on the thought board, *Who is your wolf* . . . that's an interesting thought. Can anyone tell me what might be wrong with the question?"

This is it. I watch Red. Her eyes go round as she reads the board.

"Red's wolf isn't her dad, it's the car accident," Vanet says and then jabs a thumb into his chest. "I know my wolf. Me."

Stenson smiles. "You're right, Vanet. The reason why patients arrive here is more often a *what* rather than a *who*. Yes, experiences like a car accident can be the root of some problems, but the illness is yours alone. It's internal, and something that can be treated."

"If Milly does have a wolf, it's her stepmother," Rottengoth says. "That's easy."

I flush and heat washes over me. Red's leaving in an hour or two—I need to bring to light what I think is really happening to her.

. . . "*Was* it the accident?" I ask. "I mean for Red, is the wolf the accident? I know that's what put her here, but what *keeps* her here?"

Red's eyes shine with hate and I falter. It's not what I expected from her, but it confirms my suspicions. I need to say this, or I'll forever regret it. It would be like letting Peter climb on to the roof all over again. I need to finish my count.

"Don't you dare," Red says.

But no one else talks over me. They're all respecting the count.

. . . "Why were—"

"No, Milly," Red interrupts.

It's just my OCD.

I blow past it, I have to, despite the grimy roots looping to tug at my intestines. Despite the gnarled trunks that rear up over the path, I say without counting, "Why were you in the car, Red? Where were you going with your mom?"

Panic gushes in me, the stomach clenching, then my heart and throat. I grip the edges of the chair seat and haul upward as if I might otherwise be pulled from it.

Red glances to Stenson, who is suddenly pensive and then says, "Maybe this is another discussion best had outside of group."

No one seems to have noticed that I'm exploding.

"Oh my god," Vanet says. "I get it. I think I know."

Red moans.

"Know what?" Pig asks. "If I had hair, I'd be pulling it."

"Her dad's boning her," he says.

"Vanet!" Stenson shouts.

Red crumples to the floor into a crimson ball.

I gasp for air, but everyone is watching Red.

Red sobs, then again, a deep braying sound that rounds her back. Stenson rubs her spine. She gives us the go-away look, but no one moves. Red's talking.

Red's words are garbled, but I understand them.

"He's not . . . boning me . . . but . . . ."

She makes these staccato whines as if fighting for breath. When she settles, she looks to Stenson, who nods. "You're okay. You're safe."

Red swallows. "I never know if he's going to be nice or not . . . you know? Sometimes he'd come home with flowers and chocolates and movies and we'd snuggle on the couch, all of us, my mom, my dad, me." Then her voice lowers weirdly. "Other times he'd slam the door and start punching. I'd hide." She sobs for another minute and no one says a word. "The day of the accident, my mom didn't wait for him to come home to see who would come through the door. She packed the car and we left. She was so brave. We had nothing. Then the truck hit us. We were escaping. We were finally breaking free of him. My dad's been nice ever since. So, good-dad. But I know . . . I miss her."

The last ripple of anxiety passes through me, and I release my chair seat. A tear tracks down my cheek. *I did it. I didn't die.*

"It's okay," Stenson says, rising up over Red as if she's a wolf protecting her cub. "It's okay. You're not going anywhere."

When Red looks back at me again, the hate's gone, replaced by agony.

Chapter 23

I assume the police caught up with Red's father before he made it to the ward, because I don't see him again.

A celebratory energy fills the unit now, as if things are looking up. Even Pig's happy, which is weird considering how she hasn't hidden the fact she's afraid of leaving the unit tomorrow—the denizens of her Dark Wood are all too real.

Pig keeps asking when my stepmother's coming. She *is* coming. She wants to be at my next patient meeting with Balder.

It happens before dinner. Adriana gets here way early and spends most the time talking to the nurses rather than to me. This suits me fine, because I haven't done my workbook homework.

The green tab's a worksheet titled *Panic Attack*.

So you've had a panic attack. You know, the one in which you COMPLETELY wigged out and thought you were going to kick the bucket? But you didn't; really, you won't. If you're like most cats with anxiety, you probably think a panic attack is terrible, disastrous, and that EVERYONE will laugh, and you'll NEVER pass the school year, NO ONE will like you, and you'll ALWAYS be sick. Are you catching my drift?

Write down each time you used one of those ALL CAPS words in the last few days. You might have said it. You might have thought it. Write down everything you can remember.

This is unfortunately easier than it should be.

EVERYONE will laugh at me at the dance. I'll NEVER get better. NO ONE will like me on the psych ward. I ALWAYS suck at gym.

Now in front of each sentence add, Is it likely that . . . and add a question mark at the end.

I write: Is it likely that I ALWAYS suck at gym?

Take your wiggin' out hat off for a sec and answer the question.

I write: Sometimes I'm not great at what the teacher wants us to do. Usually I'm okay, but I'm never the worst in class.

So I don't suck. Or, at least there are other kids who suck worse.

See, the problem is that you focus on the uncool rather than the gnarly other stuff you can do.

Do you remember thinking "I am going to die!?" That was a panic attack, right? It's a setback. You probably thought, "I'll NEVER get better." How much of that is your gut reaction rather than noodling about it with your brain? You may FEEL that way, but that doesn't make it so. I feel gross some mornings, but I know I'm not always gross, right?

I nod to the book.

I can't walk through a door without counting or I'll unleash the wolves.

Is it likely that I'll unleash wolves? Is it likely that I can walk through a door without counting?

My fear ratchets to an eight as my wolf watches me fight

through this. I scratch a *No* into the page, going over and over the lines until it etches through. *Not yet.*

I finish before my meeting with Balder. When I enter the interview room, Balder and my stepmother are chatting. I hop in and sit across from the doctor. I swear there's a twinkle in his eye. Adriana wrings her hands. Why she has to come to these things is beyond me. I'm sixteen. If she's brought me a birthday present, I don't see it.

"I want you to get angry," Balder says.

I lift an eyebrow. Over time, some people—those that can be my real friends—begin to read my body language rather than expect a verbal response. It's made me sensitive to the body language of others as well. I also tend to accentuate my own actions to help foster this. Balder's really in tune with me. I don't have to say a word.

"Why get angry?" he asks. "Because anxiety and anger are not compatible. Neither are anxiety and pleasure, but that's a harder emotion to force unless you take great pleasure in something like singing. You can't count and sing. They'd compete."

I shake my head emphatically. They do *not* want me singing.

"Could I give her a massage, Doctor, instead?" Adriana asks. "That might be easier for her."

I roll my eyes. Even Adriana can interpret that one.

"It's a good thought, but these coping skills are individual. In fact, many people with anxiety disorders have safe people they cling to. It's an unhealthy coping mechanism and one that I'd rather not create now by having Milly require you to massage her in order to step through a doorway."

Adriana flushes.

I nod again. I have no safe person. Well, maybe Bill. I'll do more stuff with Bill. Like dance.

"Don't get me wrong, Mrs. Malone, your instinct to protect makes sense, but it can be a negative. If someone you care about is in deep pain and all you have to do is wait with them for the pain to go away, you would, right?"

We both nod.

"Of course you would. Who cares, if waiting doesn't make sense? It solves the problem. But what if every time you did this, that person adds something new. So first it's to go through doors and you can handle that, but then it's to take a bite, and then to speak . . ."

I see where this is headed.

"Eventually," Doctor Balder continues, "there's a breaking point where there isn't enough time in the day to fit in all of these compulsions. It affects marriages, friendships, jobs. At some point you have to stop waiting with your friend, even if that means feeling like a *bad* friend."

"Or a bad stepmother," Adriana says, looking down. "I see. I've been feeding it."

Feeding the toad—the wolf.

"Good, here's what I want you to do, Milly. The next time you're about to go through a doorway, try to do so without counting." He raises a hand to forestall my response. "Yes, you will become anxious. Get mad. Shout at it. Imagine OCD as a person telling you to do the counting and tell the OCD off. Bring a pillow you can pound with your fist. Find something— not someone—you can abuse. Then when you feel as enraged as possible, step right through. If the anxiety surges, attack that pillow again."

I'm nervous and, for the first time, not only about the anxiety I expect, but also the excitement of actually doing it.

"Give it a try. How about now?" he asks.

Adriana's practically trembling, and I can see that nervousness in her she mentioned. It's mounting, rapidly.

I push back from the interview room table.

"Good, now, what would you say to your anxiety if it were a person?"

. . . "Go away?" I say.

"Yes! But with anger. GO AWAY!" His shout echoes, and I cringe. "Why do you want it to go away?"

. . . "Because it stops me from doing things." I know he'll want specifics, so I continue. "Like gym class and going shopping and having a normal conversation. It costs me friends, and good grades, and sucks up all my time . . ." I choke on the pause. It's already a lot more than I'd thought.

"Great. Go away! I want to exercise and shop, and have friends and talks! Are you ready?" Balder bounces with an energy that's contagious.

My heart starts to hammer, but it's a different feel. It's like when I was at a track meet years ago before my mom died and my teacher put me in a sprint race. At the start line my heart started to pound, and energy filled me. Positive energy that allowed me to shoot out of the blocks.

I stand in front of the doorway.

. . . "Go away," I say.

"GO AWAY!" the doctor shouts again.

. . . "You're like an anchor," I say. "You're holding me back like . . . like Velcro strips . . ." I start to laugh and then force my serious face back on. "I want to live," I whisper.

But I swear the doorway has turned from a metal frame into a guillotine.

Balder touches me on the shoulder. I jump.

"That's a really good start, really good. For your homework, I want you to find something that you can use to express your anger physically."

I take a hard look at Adriana. Too bad it has to be a some*thing*, instead of some*body*.

Doctor Balder leaves, and to my surprise, Adriana checks her watch.

"I have to go, too," she says.

. . . "Okay," I say and I'm left alone while counting . . . and on my birthday. She actually forgot.

At dinner, Pig sits right next to me. That in itself isn't unusual, but she keeps shuffling in super close. It's not until it's too late that I realize what's happening. Tink flits into the room and hums a C-note.

I should have known the nurses wouldn't forget my birthday. A small part of me didn't want them to, but most of me hates the embarrassment of being sung to by a bunch of people I don't know well. Come to think of it, though, I wonder whether I know these people better than anyone.

The rendition of Happy Birthday has to be one of the worst ever. Rottengoth sounds like he's drawing knives across his arms. I'm pretty sure Vanet believes he's an operatic star, which he certainly isn't. Tink sings in this crystalline voice, way more shrill than any fingernails on a chalkboard. Only Peter has a nice deep baritone. Pig just rubs her hands together and watches the doorway.

Adriana steps through, carrying a huge slab of cake ablaze with sixteen candles. She smiles at me, but they've turned down the lights and so her face has a campfire cast to it. The smile's wolfish. Her teeth seem sharper, and the shadows beneath her cheekbones push out her jaw. I know it's not real, but I can see it anyway.

"Happy birthday, Milly," she says after the singing settles and she slides the cake before me. Stenson hands me a plastic knife.

"Watch your hair," Pig says, her eyes lit, reflecting the flames. This is the little piggy who sees how she can be safe from the wolf. "Fire."

"Make a wish," Vanet says and then points at himself.

I don't know what to wish for. I can't have my fantasy. I don't want my dreams.

"She has to count to make wishes?" Pig rolls her eyes, but everyone else laughs. Then I blow out all the candles in one go. I'm not sure I could have done that four days ago.

"Was I your wish?" someone asks from the hallway and I whirl, because he was.

Chapter 24

"Happy birthday, honey," my dad says and steps through the doorframe.

I leap to my feet, and Pig jumps up at the same time and knocks into Adriana, who stumbles so that she braces herself using the cake, her hands sinking deep into the icing.

Pig apologizes, but I'm racing to my dad, who picks me up and hugs me.

"You didn't think I'd miss your birthday?" he says, and I laugh. "When Adriana called and told me what she'd planned, I managed an earlier flight."

"Thanks, Dad." I bury my face into his shoulder to hide my tears. It's been a tough week, a tough month.

"Shh," he says quietly.

Tink asks if anyone wants cake and is answered with a chorus of affirmations.

"I'll lick your fingers, Adriana," Pig says and, to Adriana's credit, she doesn't get angry.

"Nothing I can't take care of myself," she replies and sucks the icing off. Vanet can't tear his eyes away as she draws a finger from her lips.

"Down, son," my dad says to Vanet. I keep a tight hold on my dad's sleeve.

. . . "He's okay, Dad," I say.

I laugh again and it feels so good. It's as if the unit has lit a huge bonfire that keeps all the wolves at bay. For the next hour I grill my father on what he's done over the last two weeks and everything that's happened in the outside world since I arrived on the ward.

Doctor Balder joins us for a family meeting and introduces himself. My father's sort of roly-poly. *Stick and ball,* some kids used to call us on account of my being so thin and him having these big, round cheeks and a round belly. But it's his laughter that makes him attractive. I should have known he'd find a new wife so soon after my mother died. A guy like him needs to laugh and that means someone to share it with. I'm not known for my laughter. Even now he jokes with Balder. And I also know that his being on the chubby side is a result of all the travel he needs to do for work, bouncing from tradeshow to conference to tradeshow.

"I sure can't diagnose Milly as being boring," Doctor Balder says.

"Imagine that," my dad replies. "What would you prescribe for a compulsively boring patient? Weekly skydiving lessons and a career as a stunt actor?"

Balder laughs. "I'm afraid the skydiving instructors don't take me out to lunch like the drug reps do. So Prozac it is. I'm only kidding, of course."

"When is Milly coming home, Doctor?" my father asks. Everything feels different. Adriana was fighting to have me committed. My father wants me home. And I want to go home.

Doctor Balder sighs. "All joking aside, Milly has had some challenges. Nightmares, a setback with some of the other patients. Our job here is to stabilize her and get her home so that psychotherapy can continue on an outpatient basis, but I'd really like to have a good day with her so she can leave feeling strong."

My father's nodding. "Is that how you feel, Milly? One more day?"

"I still don't think the dance is such a great idea," Adriana says and I ignore her.

I am growing stronger, but the panic attack . . . that was like nothing I've ever experienced. And I did speak without counting today at group. I'd really like for that to happen again. As for the dance, I don't want to jinx this.

. . . "One more day," I say what everyone wants to hear. "I'll see Pig off."

"Pig?" my dad asks.

. . . "Yeah, the bald kid who ate three servings of cake."

Adriana chuckles. "I actually thought she was feeling me up. She's the one who suggested we have your party here."

We say our goodbyes and my dad promises to collect me tomorrow. On the way out a pamphlet falls out of Adriana's purse and I pick it up for her and read the title before handing it back. *A Resource for Mothers of Children with Anxiety Disorders.*

A resource for *mothers* . . . .

I meet her eyes, and she lowers them almost immediately. As the door clicks open, I hold up the pamphlet to show Adriana and ask, "Doctor Balder, what's the diagnosis for someone who believes they are someone they're not?"

He scratches his head for a second. "A delusion? They might be considered to have psychosis, but that's a broad term and symptomatic of many disorders."

"Deluded, thanks," I say, holding my stare on Adriana's back as she walks stiff spined away.

I'm buoyed by my dad having visited. The day has flown by and I hurry to the phone to call Bill.

I have to dial twice before he finally picks up. Then I rap the receiver three times so he knows it's me.

"Hey, Milly," he says. "How's the loony bin?"

My cheeks heat. I hear laughter on the other end of the line. He's being deliberately mean for their benefit.

. . . "Friends over?" I ask. "I can call back when you don't need to cater to their shallow, clichéd, ignorant and frankly boring understanding of mental illness."

There's a muffling of the receiver. It sounds as though he put his hand over it.

"Hey, sorry, I'm dealing with it," he says. "It is a little crazy, though, you know?"

. . . "You know, I don't know, because everyone here's cool. Exceptional even. Groovy."

As I'm talking Peter dances past and I have to stifle my giggles. If people on the outside danced half as much as Peter, life would be better.

"Now you're laughing at me?" Bill asks, misinterpreting. "Listen, I've had your back. Everyone here's been poking fun at you *and* me, too."

. . . "Sorry, Billy, that must be really hard." I say it like I mean it, but I don't. I really don't.

"Are you going to the dance, or what?" he asks.

I look up to the ceiling and draw a deep breath. He apologized, and if he has had my back, that's cute.

. . . "Do you want to go to the dance with me?" I ask.

He stammers as he says, "Well, you sure it's a good idea, with the panic attacks and everything?"

I never told him about the attack.

I give up.

"No," I say. "I'm going to hang here." I'm already regretting saying to my dad that I should stay. I should have left and gone to the dance. Alone. That's therapy.

"Oh, good," he replies. "Your stepmom will be pretty happy about that."

Even if I wasn't a counter, I'd still need to take a moment to control myself before answering.

. . . "What?" I ask. "My stepmom's been talking to you?"

"Yeah, about the dance, you know, and trying to make sure I understand what's going on." To my silence he adds, "She only wants what's best for you. She's really worried."

. . . "Yeah, worried I'll get out of here and ruin her life."

I hang up.

Chapter 25

I seethe. I can't seem to stop clenching my hands into fists. I retreat to my room, where I pick up the ping-pong ball and imagine it to be Adriana's head before squeezing it. It's a *something*, right? It can be my punching bag. I can't focus on homework and end up talking to Beauty.

. . . "Bill doesn't want me to go to the dance with him," I say. That much was pretty clear to me; what's not as clear is why. "It's not only Adriana. He's totally embarrassed to be dating a crazy chick. Well, he doesn't need to worry about that anymore, does he?" We hadn't been going out for very long; it was a lot to expect him to handle.

Beauty says nothing.

. . . "I don't think I'm overreacting," I say, poking at her shoulder. "If I were smart, I'd go anyway and show Bill and Adriana what I think of their concern. Maybe I can talk to Bill there. Make up with him, if he sees me. I hate the telephone."

Sleeping Beauty stays silent and imperious.

. . . "It's not a bad idea. What's the worst that can happen? They put me back in here, right? It's not against the law for me to leave the hospital, or anything. They'd be pissed, but—"

Sleeping Beauty sighs.

. . . "I don't really care what you think." A slow smile spreads across my face. "What's the craziest thing you've ever done, Milly?" It would be nice to have a real answer to that question like: Escaped the psych ward.

Sleeping Beauty's expression remains flat and uncaring. She doesn't believe I'll do it. That I *can* do it.

I sag onto the edge of her mattress. She's right. It's one thing to have a crazy idea, it's wholly another to figure out how to execute it. It's too late in the day to be discharged now, and the dance starts in less than an hour, so if I were going to do this, I'd have to figure out how to sneak out of here on my own. The thought sends blood pounding in my head. Maybe Bill *is* my safe person.

Vanet walks past the room as I'm about to speak.

. . . "Ha! Just what I need, a fairy godmother. Vanet?" I call, and he peeps inside. I wave him closer and his head swings left and right before entering.

"Now we're talking," he says.

. . . "I want to ask you a question." The way his face droops would be comical if it weren't so predictable; it does make me pause long enough that I have to count.

"Oh, oh!" He waves his hands in front of my face. "Wait."

I count more slowly.

From his pockets, he pulls three tennis balls. He gets two going, but when he adds the third, they bounce all over the place. "I can do it," he says. "I've done it. Wait."

He snatches up the balls and starts again, two and then a third. "Gimme a fourth, I want a fourth."

He's doing it, he really is, the balls are looping in the air, but Vanet always wants more. I glance around, but the only thing I see is Pig's pencil sharpener. I hold it up.

"Perfect. On three," he says. "One, two, three!"

I lob it into the air. He doesn't even try, whirls on his toes and smacks the balls. The balls and sharpener fly in all directions, pencil shavings scatter. He stands there, grinning. "I did it. Told you I would. Now what is your fervent wish?"

He glances for the balls again and I kick the nearest away.

. . . "How would you break out of here, if you needed to?"

He thinks about that. "Opportunity or emergency," he says. "Either you wait for an opportunity like Peter took with the lunch lady, or you create an emergency and slip out in the confusion. Like your panic attack. I could have left a dozen times, the door was opening and closing like Pig's legs."

Nice.

"Where are we going?" he asks. "I accept your kind, if rather desperate, invitation."

. . . "You don't even know what I'm doing. And I'm not desperate."

He shrugs as if this is the least of his worries. "I stay, I play ping-pong. I go, maybe I can get down your pants."

Why did I ask him? Because he's the opposite of Bill. . . . "Promise not to do anything crazy?" I wince even as I say it.

He salutes. "So where *are* we going?"

. . . "Better put your dancing shoes on," I say.

"Awesome." His eyes light and he rolls his hands before sticking his arm up in a classic disco move. "I'm such a good dancer."

I sigh. I'm the crazy one for asking him.

. . . "On one condition—you have to help me get out of here," I say.

"Your wish is my command. Be ready for anything."

. . . "And, Vanet, it's a costume party."

He skips out of the room. I can't believe I told Vanet. I feel light-headed; I feel free. And nervous. Very nervous. Like vomit-nervous. This time it's totally rational. After sweeping up as much of the pencil shavings as I can with my bare hands, I go through my clothes. Of course, Adriana didn't provide anything suitable for a dance, but I do have a sheer camisole that goes well with a silk skirt. I put them on and then throw jeans and a shirt over the top. I don't want anyone asking too many questions. Then I pocket some of Red's very red lipstick. We haven't spoken directly since I spilled the beans on her father's abuse. I hope she won't mind my borrowing her lipstick.

I can, however, spend some time on my hair. I brush it out and then braid it into a crown.

Vanet knocks on the side of the doorframe and whispers, "Start counting now."

It's eight p.m. Vanet has not tried for low-key in his clothing choices. He's dressed to the nines, wearing a shirt that's a cross between chainmail and a mirror. His black jeans are so tight he must have spent the last hour getting them on, and his hair is gelled up in a faux-hawk. Pretty sure his skin is sparkling too. He's got a plastic bag full of something.

I'm out the door of my room and standing in the hallway.

Then there's screaming like I've never heard before. Vanet winks as he jogs down the hall from the acute room to grip my hand. Wolfgang bangs at his door, even though he can open it all by himself. Nurses scramble and a code is called.

"Code white," Stenson says over the PA speaker.

When the outer door clicks open, two orderlies blow past and we curl out, me with the smallest of hops. The whole time I'm squeezing that ping-pong ball like mad. At the end of the hall, the elevator doors are open and we slide right inside.

"Poop bomb," Vanet says, but I'm preparing to count to leave the elevator so his words barely register. "I tossed a poop bomb at Wolfgang."

Elevators are tricky and, leaving it, Vanet has to hold the door open until I finish the count while the elevator car alarm buzzes in protest. Then I give another tiny hop. No one notices, but this is a hospital and patients come in all shapes, sizes, and degrees of bizarre. Soon enough we're counting toward the exit. I break all sorts of counting rules, rushing and counting in my head.

When we finally reach the taxi stop, my mouth's dry from my near-constant whispering.

"So what's the craziest thing you've ever done?" Vanet asks. And I laugh and give him a high-five.

. . . "It wasn't a real poop-bomb, right? That would send Wolfgang over the edge." I'm concerned; Vanet has a habit of pushing things. "What was in the plastic bag?"

"Your leftover chocolate birthday cake," he says, and holds the door to the taxicab wide open. "Happy birthday, Milly. Tonight, I am your disco dancing fairy godmother."

Chapter 26

I keep glancing back to the hospital doors, expecting a platoon of orderlies to burst out bearing long needles. While the driver waits for directions, Vanet explains that I have trouble getting words out. The driver starts the meter.

"We're eloping," Vanet says, taking advantage of my silence. "Young love, you know? Who would have thought we would have found it in here? But we did, except she has an inoperable brain tumor and I have this disease where my heart is too big from being so full of love. We both only have days to live, but that's our infinity, right?"

. . . "Hopedell High School, don't believe a word he says."

"Don't leave me at the altar, Guinevere, not like the last time." Vanet clutches his chest in mock agony.

The driver ignores us and turns out of the hospital drive.

From his bag Vanet pulls a doctor's long, white coat and a stethoscope. It's perfect and simple. I take off my sweater and my jeans, which have bunched up my skirt. Vanet lifts his eyebrows suggestively and I shake my head, putting on the costume. I'm terrified and excited.

. . . "We're staying for one hour, no more," I tell him. "I—"

"You don't have to explain anything to me, I've watched Cinderella *so* many times," Vanet says. "Besides, I know what we're doing. You want to make Bill jealous. Just you wait."

Is that what I want? No.

. . . "Really, I only want to prove to everyone I'm normal. I'm still just me."

"Unlike me, who is not so normal," he says.

. . . "I—you know what? I wish I were a bit more like you. I really do. I wish everyone was."

He bursts into a grin. "Then tonight, Doctor Malone, you will have that chance."

Ten minutes later we roll into the school parking lot.

Other kids are hanging out beside cars. Some wear costumes, mostly *Scream* masks and devil's horns. I cringe at a wolf's head. Someone hides a bottle; another, a rolled cigarette. Vanet insists on paying for the taxi, and I ask the driver if he can come back in an hour. It feels better to have a deadline, but the driver tells me to call the company when I'm ready.

When I step out of the cab, nothing happens. The students return to their furtive drinking and smoking. I catch a scarecrow's whisper, but maybe it's not about me. After all, Vanet's wearing a disco ball shirt. He comes around and threads an arm through mine, escorting me inside, slowing before we hit a doorway to allow me time to count. I feel wolfish eyes burn at my back. Our entry is seamless. As I pass my locker, I count to open it and stash my clothes.

A teacher chaperon does a double-take when we skip into the gym, but that's it. It's totally normal.

And then Vanet starts bopping to the beat.

"Did I mention," he says, shouting over the music, "that I'm the winner of many dance competitions?"

I'm shaking my head, and I suspect he's assuming I'm shaking it because I didn't know this wonderful fact, not shaking my head to say, *Please do NOT do this.*

The dance started about an hour ago, but aside from a few feet-shufflers on the outskirts and a giggling troupe of freshmen in a corner—two ghosts, six witches, five cats, a Batman, two Supermen, and a Wolverine—the stage is Vanet's. At first Vanet's funny, doing a disco routine and then some moves I don't know the names for, but where he looks like a robot, an ancient Egyptian, or old-school Michael Jackson. Other kids have noticed, and I see they've made the connection between me and Vanet anyway, so I try to ignore the hollow feel of my stomach and join him. I copy the popping of his chest and shoulders, and he tries to teach me a routine, but it's no good. He is actually not bad—not competition good or anything, but you can tell he's spent too much time in front of the mirror practicing this stuff.

Not only can I not hear a word he's saying over the music, but I'm also nearly consumed by laughter half the time. I'm having more fun than I can remember having. Ever.

Like every school dance I've been to, the DJ has no sense of timing. A critical mass of students has finally found the dance floor, but on comes some slow song to drive most of them back to the bleachers. I'm about to head over to the side of the gym when Vanet snatches my hand and pulls me into him. His cologne rolls over me, but I don't resist.

I haven't counted in half an hour. Not once. There's been no need. I've decided that I don't have to count to laugh. And it's weird because with Bill, I'm always counting, even when I don't need to. Just in case. Just in case he says something to me and I want to seem as normal as possible by replying as quickly as I can. A rolling count, counting to speak—but having nothing to say.

. . . "You are crazy," I say to Vanet. "In a really good way."

His response is to grab my butt, so I brush his hand away. Students chat on the bleachers, but the one in the wolf mask stares. I shake it off. Who knows what the kid's looking at beneath the dollar-store plastic? Vanet and I dance for another minute, holding each other. His wiry muscles pressed against me. If this kid can get his meds balanced, he'll take over the world. I feel a sense of loss when the DJ begins to lay a heavy bass over the slow music. Vanet winks at me as we move apart, cooler air swirling between us. I've done what I came to do. To have some fun. To prove I could. To challenge authority, especially Adriana's. I feel a little wild. A little like I've reclaimed some of the Dark Wood. The only person I haven't seen is Bill, but why would he come without me?

The drinking and smoking-up kids start to wind their way into the gym, and the DJ further ramps the music. A circle forms and a group of kids dressed as skeletons with glow-in-the-dark bones start showing off their skill. They're the school's hip-hop group and call themselves the Skeleton Crew. Vanet pushes his way to the circle's edge, hooting at the tight moves and applauding.

. . . "We should go," I call.

"A few more minutes," he says, and he's been so great that I relent.

With all his antics and the shirt, Vanet's hard to miss and finally one of the crew pops his chest out at Vanet and gives him the floor he so obviously covets.

. . . "Don't, Vanet," I shout. "Please. We should go." I really don't want him to do this to himself—the night's been so much fun, and I don't want to wreck it.

Vanet doesn't look back. He strides into the center. The Skeleton Crew postures with calculated indifference. People clap to the beat. Only Vanet's shoulders move as if he draws the throbbing heart of the music into him.

That's when I catch sight of Bill on the opposite side, the wolf mask pushed up onto his forehead. He would have seen me arrive with Vanet. Dancing with Vanet. *Slow* dancing with Vanet. And now he's pointing at Vanet and laughing.

Then . . . then Vanet goes insane.

Chapter 27

During the Olympics I like to watch gymnastics. It never ceases to amaze me how strong someone can be. Vanet's like a gymnast. He does a flip from a stand. The circle grows wider and a huge cheer goes up. My jaw drops with the Skeleton Crews'. Vanet begins in earnest, and I can't peel my eyes away even to find Bill.

Vanet spins on his back, legs flaring and windmilling, until he shoots up into a one-handed handstand before spinning again, flipping up off the floor from his back. I cheer. It shrieks from my mouth. No counting.

People are going mad, pumping their fists. Vanet runs, jumps, and slides his head along the ground, feet to the ceiling, sending girls shrieking. A delirious grin paints his face. Sparkles blaze from his shirt and I feel as though we're orbiting him.

Again he spins on his back, and then on his head before flopping onto his front like a corpse.

There's a burst of applause. The whole routine took no more than a few minutes, but no one steps up to follow it. No one goes in to replace him—who could?—but my smile falters when Bill holds out a hand to help him up.

I rush forward, but everyone's backslapping Vanet and pushing closer to . . . I dunno what they're trying to do . . . touch him? Sweat shakes from his hair, which now points in all directions.

. . . "Vanet!" I call, but the shout is lost to the beat of a new song. I jostle someone.

"Hey, Mill, heard you were in the hospital." It's Stephanie, the video-everything chick. I try to ignore her, but she's whipped out her phone. It's in my face. "This is Steph Lattersby, reporting from Hopedell High School where Milly Ma—"

"What do you plan to do with that?" I demand without counting, sensing that I'm burning through a valuable reservoir within me. "You want my picture? To video me counting before I respond?" I'm screaming now. "Listen, snot-smear, if you had any inkling of what some people go through . . . if you thought for just a second about the chick on the other side of that screen. You wouldn't do that."

She's dropped her arm and the phone to her side.

I ignore her open mouth, and push forward. That felt good, but everything's too close. Pressing. Vanet's moved farther away, drawn by Bill and several others, the Screams and the scarecrow from the parking lot. Vanet's nodding, his eyes bright with glee. He bounces with each step. Bill marches. Only once does Bill glance to me and then to Vanet. Bill's back goes ramrod straight and his jaw sets. I've always loved that jaw, but now its hard line stabs fear through me. Bill's friends nudge shoulders with fists and give nods before following on behind their leader; the pack hunts. The wolf mask gloats back at me. Everyone smiles at the teacher at the rear exit of the gym, and then they're through. I must count. Refuel.

My hour's almost up. The night nurse will have checked our rooms long before now. A code will have been called. What was I thinking? And what's Billy doing with Vanet?

I hop through the doorframe, sighing at the odd look I get from the teacher.

Bill took this route on purpose, trying to slow me down. It has so many doorways. Anger burbles in my gut. I have three more doors to pass, the set of mid-hallway fire doors, another at the stairwell, and a final one to reach outside. I have to count. But Vanet can't afford that. My hands clench into fists. I flex my jaw and get down in a sprinter's crouch. I'm angry at myself, but I'm enraged at Billy. And anxiety isn't compatible with rage.

Ready. Set. Go!

I blast through the fire doors, the same ones I'd cringed at with Stephanie and her video. I can't tell if my racing heart is a panic attack or adrenaline. Another hundred feet, and I careen off one wall, hit a set of lockers, and then my shoulder hits the stairwell door. The walls, ceiling, and floor constrict. I kick the last door open before tumbling into the night air.

On my knees, I draw too-quick, too-short breaths. I have to count. I'm too late.

Vanet's up against the school yard brick wall, beneath which I shoot hoops and play twenty-one. Two guys hold Vanet's arms while Bill faces off. Now *his* feet bounce; he's filled with energy.

"Go away, Milly," Bill says.

My eyes narrow, but I'm whispering away the panic in my guts, damming an eruption of bile.

"You've got time, she's counting," one of his friends says and then laughs.

Vanet's eyes roll with fear. I brought him here. This is my fault. Everything is my fault.

"I need to teach him not to move in on another guy's girlfriend," Bill says by way of explanation. He wipes sweat from his forehead.

No, not everything's my fault.

"What?" I ask. "You're going to beat him up?"

Bill hesitates. "Is this guy one of them?" He must read the question marks blazing in my eyes. "One of the psych kids. He is, isn't he?"

I can't count. It will steel Bill's resolve. "So what if he is?" I make it to my feet, but the tightening of my chest tries to anchor me. I stagger forward.

"I was only going to scare him." Bill throws up his hands. "Listen, I didn't ask for all of this. You were quirky, that's all. Not this."

I push past Bill and shove aside the scarecrow and Scream-mask who hold Vanet. I grab his hand and pull him toward the front of the school.

"You're an idiot and you're not my boyfriend," I say to Bill.

I won't say that it doesn't hurt, but Bill's made this a really easy breakup. I can't believe I thought I was falling for him. I think I wanted to fall for anyone who thought I was girlfriend material. Something Balder said surfaces in my brain: Anxiety isn't compatible with pleasure either. I don't think I can have a real boyfriend—a good one—until I can control my anxiety.

"Crazy bitch," Bill says to my back, and I raise my hand and give him the finger.

Wait. I can do more. I stop and turn. "Crazy bitch?" I realize that I spoke again without counting, and parts of the wood that I'd thought reclaimed send tendrils and suckers up from razed stumps to curl about my heart.

It's my OCD. But I need to do this. Not for fear, not to protect Vanet, but for me this time.

Bill and his henchmen freeze. "Yeah," Bill says.

"What's the evidence for this?" I say. But I will not count.

Vanet barks a laugh.

"How about you in a lunatic asylum bringing another psycho-boyfriend to the dance?" Bill says.

"Are you looking at the whole picture?" I ask, to which I get a quizzical stare. "I mean, you didn't want to come with me. Yet you showed up alone. And you never once saw us so much as kiss. What evidence do you have that I'm seeing him? That I'm the bitch when you're a liar?"

"You're still crazy," he says, folding his arms.

Vanet winks at me.

"Yeah, well, we all are a bit," I say.

"Thank God for that," Vanet replies.

I turn away and snatch Vanet's hand again.

"I could have taken them," Vanet says as we fast-walk away. "I'm the intercontinental kickboxing champion."

"We can go back," I reply.

"Nah, wouldn't want to ruin my shirt." I laugh and he laughs too. "Hey! You're not counting."

"But I want to *so* bad," I say.

"Nicely done."

"I can't believe I ever liked him."

"Amazing what we can convince ourselves of."

We're quiet while we march beside the school. When we reach the front, the taxi's waiting even though we never called, and we get inside. With the door shut, my body leaves attack mode and I sag. Vanet turns to me and says, "That was so totally worth it. Didn't I say I can dance?"

"You can so dance, Vanet, so dance." And I kiss him on the cheek.

Chapter 28

Stenson faces us as Vanet walks and I skip through the psych ward door. The first thing I notice is that the ward's busy. It's almost like daytime despite it being late. A police officer's at the nursing station. The lights are on and blinding, rather than the usual dimmers used at night. A shout goes up as we enter, reminding me of the cheer at Vanet's surprise flip on the dance floor, but the joy sours.

Behind the nursing station glass, Tink collapses into tears. Stenson doesn't show any pleasure at our arrival, expression shifting from flat to volcanic in a flash.

"This them?" the police officer says and then scribbles a note on a pad, before shaking his head and leaving.

Stenson pulls us both into interview room one and erupts. "How could you?"

Despite her face being a twisted scowl, I don't see a witch. I see an angry nurse. A betrayed nurse.

"No, don't count, don't speak—listen." She pauses as if daring us to say something. "This ward is a place of healing. It is a place of trust. Break that trust and you break our ability to heal.

You may be willing to ruin this for yourselves, but I will not let you ruin it for others. Wolfgang . . ." Her voice cracks, and she draws a deep breath. "After you pulled your stunt, Wolfgang required chemical restraints." I swallow hard. This was me. It was all me. "What were you thinking?"

Vanet begins to say something, but I grab his arm and he quiets.

. . . "I'm sorry, Nurse Stenson," I say. "I'm really sorry. The whole thing was my idea. I was upset with my boyfriend. With my stepmom. I wanted to prove to them I wasn't crazy."

The nurse shuts her eyes. "No one here is *crazy*," she says. "You should have realized that by now. You have nothing to prove. You come here when you are sick. You leave when you are better."

"I want her home tonight." My father stands in the doorway. "She hasn't been fair to the other patients."

Beside him Adriana is barred entry by his arm. She's got one leg into the room.

"I can appreciate that," Stenson replies to my dad. "But I'd prefer to discharge her in the morning. To be honest, I'd like to get home and sleep, and having Milly pack up now would be highly disruptive to the other patients."

"I'm sorry, Daddy," I say and tears well in my eyes.

"She can pack up tomorrow," my dad says.

Stenson regards him and shakes her head. "It's your choice, but I would prefer we let Milly sleep here tonight."

My dad stares at me and finally nods.

Adriana ducks under my father's arm to embrace me. "We were so worried," she says.

. . . "Right," I reply, prying her arms off of me. My tears turn from shame to anger. "So worried that what? I'd be allowed to come home tonight? That I'm well enough to go to the dance?"

I'm tired of her being so fake. She doesn't care.

"That's not fair, Milly," my father says. "It's about time that you start to realize what Adriana is to us."

. . . "To you," I shout.

Adriana starts crying.

"No, Milly, this whole business is on you, and the sooner you take responsibility, the sooner you can begin to realize that the people around you love you."

"This is not the time." Stenson holds up her hands, but it's as though she isn't even there.

. . . "She's only being nice to me for you," I say.

"You don't know what being nice is! Do you remember your mother? Do you? Do you *really*, Milly?"

I shut up. Blood flees to my core and I grow cold. The walls bleed to gray.

I'm stunned and I think my father is too. No one else could understand what is passing between us. What my father means. What I know, but have been holding back these years. The truth *does* always come out, like the hunter's bones by the river.

At the funeral, everyone spoke so well of my mom. *Moral, a-good-person, with-so-much-potential, a-wonderful-mother, she-is-missed.* But she wasn't. She isn't. I've been taught not to speak ill of the dead. But if my mom was so cruel, then why the dreams? Why is she always protecting me from the wolf?

"Milly and Vanet have been found safe and sound," Nurse Stenson fills the silence. "And important to healing is a good night's sleep. I'm afraid there's small chance of that now, but we can do our best."

Adriana steps forward to hug me again, and I push back up against the wall. Finally, she lets her arms drop and returns to my father. They leave.

"Clingy, that one," Vanet says.

. . . "Yeah," I whisper. "Like Saran Wrap."

"Bed," Stenson says. "We'll finish this in the morning."

With my anger spent and my head a confusion of thoughts, I need to count for the doorway. Stenson's never shown impatience for my counting, but she does now. Air whistles heavily out of her nose as she taps her bicep. Maybe she thinks I should be over it. I figured I would be by the time I was being discharged, but all the staff seems to care about is that I'm up a few pounds and my meds aren't giving me side effects.

When I'm halfway through my count, Stenson says to me, "Did you know that in the original fairy tales—not the ones told by Disney, the first versions recorded by the Grimm brothers—in Snow White and Hansel and Gretel, it wasn't an evil stepmother? It was an evil mother. They later changed them to an evil stepmother." She doesn't wait for a response. "No teeth brushing, just climb into bed," she says after me and then shuts the door.

After the light in the hall, the bedroom's pitch black. I stand waiting for my eyes to adjust. I pick out Sleeping Beauty's snores. Red tosses and turns, but no more than usual, maybe less. Pig's staring at the ceiling and gives a small wave. With the major objects in the room having taken shape, I navigate without bumping into anything, pull back my covers and slide into bed.

After the night's events, I don't expect to fall asleep quickly. But I do. And I regret it.

Stenson hasn't gone home. She sits in the nursing station, waiting for the orderlies to disappear and for Tink to settle and leave. After everyone has departed, her mask comes away. I watch as she scratches at the edge of her hairline with her fingernails, catches an edge, and peels the skin from her skull.

Beneath the skin crawl tiny maggots. They drip from her face, puffing into wisps of urine-colored smoke as they hit the desk. Always there are more. Scraggly hair writhes. Scales drop from her eyes and they stare, iris-less, white orbs, seeing, but unseeing. She opens her mouth to utter a cackle, revealing a snaking tongue and a mouth filled with rows of red teeth. But more has changed. It's not Stenson.

Now it's my mother staring at the door to 3A. She wields a sword, and I know what it's for. The thorny vine, the studded leather, the chain, nothing has stopped the wolf. The sword edge gleams with promised blood.

The wolf slides beneath Wolfgang's door and coalesces. It growls and sniffs at the air.

I know I am sleeping. I know I am sleeping and I cannot get away. My mother pushes back from the desk and pauses before the door to my bedroom, sword held out and back, ready to strike. The wolf snarls and pads down the hallway. She swings, a test. It earns her a bark and flash of curved fangs.

Should I count? For what? To protect my mother? For her to die?

She leaps forward, thrusting the tip of the blade and inflicting a glancing blow on the shoulder of the wolf. It yelps. It hops back and then immediately forward again, evading a backhand to catch my mother's wrist in its jaws. She screams and stumbles back to crack her skull against the nursing station glass. She crumples.

The wolf slinks back to 3A. It snuffles at the crack beneath my bedroom door, and then enters like steam. The giant head twists one way and then the next. It snarls back at the doorway, baring teeth. Then it whips around and launches at Pig, tearing at her blankets as she screams. It digs and digs until it finds whatever is buried there and chews it to splinters. It's something I suspected was there, like my harbored guilt. Something we all should have guessed. But dreams aren't real, and I'm too late.

I can't move. I'm terrified to attract the wolf's attention. But eventually it leaves the scattered fragments to sniff at my blankets. It rests its snout on my bed and peers at me, pink tongue rolling in and out of its mouth as if it can taste me on the air. The eyes are liquid and warm. Then a huge paw flops onto the bed, and another. With a delicate jump, it hops beside me, curling into my stomach like lovers spoon. I smell the fur's musk. It smells a little like Adriana, but mostly of smoke.

It's protecting me. It knows about my mother. Had the wolf *ever* attacked me in my dreams? . . . No. It had attacked Red and Pig, my book and Stenson, whenever I feared them, but never me. And my mother? She'd always been there to try to stop it. The wolf *protects* me.

Suddenly the wolf begins to growl. It digs at my chest, claws raising red welts. Its maw dips to my neck, jaws opening and closing over my throat.

So much for that theory.

Chapter 29

I wake beneath the wolf's nibbling teeth.

Smoke roils across the ceiling, orange and black. I cough. The wolf's gone. Why had it attacked? But now fully awake, I have bigger problems than dream interpretation. I'm on my knees, on my bed, breathing deeply of heavy fumes.

Fire lights the room. Pig's bed blazes. Flames lick the ceiling. I cry out. The spine of my book of tales disappears in the furious heat.

She used it and all our homework for kindling.

"Red," I scream. "Wake up!"

Red flips her blankets back. "What the hell?" she shouts and swings to the opposite side of her bed. "Fire!" she yells and then breaks into a coughing fit.

Someone must have tampered with the smoke detectors, because they should be blaring by now.

Heat tightens my skin and I feel my hair curl. Flames flow across the ceiling in waves. When Red flees through the door, the sudden blast of fresh air ignites a fireball. I drop to the floor as the hospital alarm sounds. All patients are directed to evacuate in an orderly fashion.

I shake Beauty, but she's groggy and red from heat, or maybe that's simply the glow of the flames on her skin.

. . . "Wake up!" Her eyes flutter. I pull her to the ground. We need to pass Pig's bed to reach the doorway and it's an inferno. Where is Pig now? I know why she did this. It all makes perfect sense and in some ways was predictable. Pig doesn't want to leave. She's safe here. So what does she need to do to stay? Light fires. Bring the police. Bring the fire department. Bring the full force of the law down upon herself. I wonder if I'm so predictable. I hear shouting in the hallway, Wolfgang versus the night nurse.

The door is so close to Pig's bed that I worry I won't be able to both haul Beauty behind me and count to cross the threshold before bursting into flames. But I must. Last night I'd been angry and pushed through without my count, but I'm not angry anymore. I'm terrified. And anxiety and fear are best friends.

I try to time my count. But each time I pull on Beauty I whine a little, so have to start counting again. The smoke itches at my throat and I choke. It's no use even starting until I'm closer to the door. I maneuver behind Beauty's head and hook arms beneath her armpits. Then with my legs I push myself backward, sliding my butt and Beauty across the floor. This is faster than pulling on her arm, but still I grunt with each push.

I'm roasting. My lungs are searing. The Dark Wood burns. Trunks tumble across the path. Tears dry on my cheeks. Then my back's up against the door. I start my count. But I'm dying in here. My count isn't saving anyone. Not me, not Sleeping Beauty. I reach back and twist the doorknob. The metal sears my fingers and I cry out, interrupting the count. The door opens.

My throat tightens, but that could be from the smoke, not my OCD. The pounding of my heart could be from the fire and the desire to live, not my OCD. This terror is rational. I slump across the threshold, pulling Beauty with me into the red-lit hall. Throat too raw to shout, I start toward the exit, which flies open. The night nurse kneels beside me. It's Stenson. She stayed. She's shouting something. I've started counting again, and I'm not done when a masked firefighter charges into the ward. What's the worst that can happen? Hasn't it happened? Isn't it happening right now? Aren't I handling it?

I think of something to get angry about, a ping-pong ball to squeeze—at first Adriana's face appears, but soon it morphs into the tense, disappointed expression of my mother. *It was an evil mother. I can tell you no more.* What has my count ever done for me? I *am* angry. I'm angry with myself, angry that I left so much of my guilt and shame at Adriana's feet, like some cat dropping a half-eaten rat on the doorstep.

I don't struggle as I'm pulled across the blissfully cool hall. Wolfgang fights orderlies who try to pull him from his room.

. . . "It's okay, Wolfgang," I rasp, and then to the orderlies I shout, "Just leave him alone, he doesn't like people touching him. Let him walk out on his own."

I don't know what happens, because I'm yanked over the psychiatric unit's threshold. Strong hands take me into their arms and pass me back to another who carries me and runs me past one threshold after another, so many doors, too many to count. I cry the entire time, open to panic that never takes hold. And then I land on a stretcher somewhere with air that's at first wonderfully cooling, but a place that soon makes me quake as a crowd of white coats press to assess my condition. An oxygen mask slides over my face. Then Stenson's back, watching. I'm Gretel and I've escaped the witch's oven. I laugh into the mask at the ridiculous thought and she smiles.

The white coats thin and I can see Beauty on a stretcher beside me. She's awake, similarly masked, and looking at me. Her eyes are so blue.

"The nurse says you saved me," she says, the sound muffled.

. . . "Tried to," I reply.

"Thank God."

. . . "Yeah," I say.

"You're a brave girl." Stenson looms closer. I turn my head, feeling my skin crackle like I have a bad sunburn.

. . . "Is Wolfgang okay?" I ask.

"He was well away from the fire," Stenson replies. "It never spread."

. . . "Pig?"

"The police have Pig."

. . . "She's safe then," I say. She got her wish. And then I sit forward with a realization. "My stepmom, Adriana, the matches were hers. Pig bumped into her and I bet Pig pocketed the matches then. The whole birthday party was only for her to get the matches."

Stenson's lips tighten.

We sit for a while. People mill, waiting for the firefighters to give the all-clear. I already know there's no going back for me and likely not for the whole unit. I scan for Vanet, but don't see him. With relief I realize he'll have made it, if the fire was confined to my room.

Stenson's on her phone, calling other hospitals, searching for patient beds. At least on the gurney, I can try to sleep. When I roll back over, something digs into my hip. I slide fingers down into my pocket and come out with the ping-pong ball. Adriana's head. I grin at it. It wasn't Adriana I imagined, though, was it? It was my mother.

I try going to my relaxed place, the raft at my grandparents'. I clench my hands, then my forearms and biceps. I sink into the mattress, the frantic world sliding by, people slowly threading back into the hospital. What was it about my grandparents' cottage that made it so peaceful? I could easily say it was the lake or the sun, but that wasn't it. My mom wasn't there. She set my teeth on edge. All this time my mother *never* had my back. Even in my dreams.

Red comes to my side. I can hear Stenson admonishing her for waking me, and trying to keep the ward together, but she can't. Not if Pig's gone and Beauty and I are here.

"They don't have a bed for me," Red says. "I'm going to a group home this morning. My dad won't even know where I live. Can you believe it?"

And it's morning. A fringe of sky lightens over the trees that border the parking lot. The lot is a sea of beds and patients.

. . . "Are you okay?" I ask, lifting my mask and propping myself up on elbows. My voice is hoarse from the smoke.

"I hope so. I mean, I'm scared about what it'll be like, but I don't want to go home either. So I'm . . . hopeful," Red says; she hasn't twitched once. "It's what my mom wanted. It's all she wanted. For me to have a chance."

I wonder if I ever really knew what my mom wanted. What

would she want for me? Too much. The wolf was trying to protect me. I can see that now. It smelled of Adriana. *It was an evil mother,* Stenson said of fairy tales. Stenson hadn't seen an overprotective bitch in Adriana. She'd seen a caring person. I had twisted everything Adriana did into something evil—and polished away the tarnish from the memory of my mom. It seems like a year ago that Balder told me how we can hold mistaken beliefs.

Vanet approaches, trailed by Peter and a glum Rottengoth. But Vanet isn't his usual blustery self; his steps are hesitant. We shared something last night, and I suspect that he doesn't want it to be over.

"You all right?" he asks.

I nod. . . . "Yeah."

"Stenson's arranging for beds. I might be discharged," he says.

. . . "You know," I say. "We could all keep in touch, right? I mean, the next time any of us get in here, we could even meet up."

"Me, too?" Peter asks.

"Of course, my man!" Vanet says and puts his arm around the big kid's waist. "Just don't jump off anything taller than you to make it happen."

Seeing Vanet embrace Peter, and with Rottengoth looking on with the hint of a smirk, I understand what makes this cool. Even though this sucks, we all are sucking together.

I smile and ask Nurse Stenson for a paper and pen, and each of us writes our email addresses on it. I promise to send an email around. Vanet smiles at me, but it's not the crazy grin. It's a quieter confidence.

"This sounds like you're asking me out on a date," he says hopefully.

. . . "Um—well, no," I say and let my hand drop. "But I could use some really good friends. Friends who don't mind a few quirks."

"Quirks are the best," he replies.

Adriana's face appears in the crowd. Tears stain her cheeks, and her eyes are so tired they seem to droop. She shoves her way through and everyone takes the hint to disappear.

"I'm so sorry," she says and folds into me, burrowing onto my gurney like the wolf had my bed. I'd known that she was the wolf before I admitted it to myself. Who had I counted for during my panic attack? Me? No—Adriana. Did I have evidence that Adriana was evil? Had she been evil to me in the past? Was I being objective?

No.

No.

No.

Tears well in my eyes and drip onto the forearm she has wrapped around my chest.

"Are you okay, honey?" Adriana asks. "I hope you're okay."

. . . "I'm sorry," I say, but my voice quavers and I can't help the tears that come because I'm not okay.

I thought I'd killed my mom. I'd wanted her to *go away* and she did.

And I must have been saying so aloud, because Adriana cuddles me.

"I know, honey, it's okay, it wasn't your fault. It's not your fault."

I clutch tight to her shoulders. My father isn't here. My stepmother is. My wolf. Protecting me as my mother never had.

"I love you," she says.

I draw a breath. A stomach breath. And I sag into her amidst the crazy scene, the crazy kids, and I'm ready to enter the crazy Dark Wood world.

That day, the girl sharpened a hunting knife; she shouldered a quiver of arrows and strung a bow of yew. That day, the girl gave up her magic and hunted the hunter. Into the Dark Wood, she slunk and laid claim to it for her own.

. . .

Acknowledgements

My last couple of books have been an exploration of fear, managing fear, where fear comes from, how it can be healthy, and how it can be a barrier to life. With Counting Wolves, I wanted to address fear in a common and challenging form, as a psychiatric disorder. I hope what makes this story relatable is that we've all faced crushing anxiety, perhaps not to Milly's degree, but we've all faced it somewhere on the continuum between lying on the dock in the sunlight while the water laps, to heart attack zone, paralyzed and wishing nothing more than to stay in bed. I'm sure I got parts of this wrong, and I accept full responsibility for those but, for the parts I got right, I need to say thank you.

Clare Roscoe, thank you for your support and for sharing your expertise. To Andrea Stewart, in all your capacities, as subject matter expert and first reader. For story, Catherine Adams of Inkslinger Editing, you called this book an old friend, and I consider you a friend too. Thank you. To my literary agent and champion, Gina Panettieri, you push me to greater heights and show me how to get there. To Julia Craig for the best beta read ever. To Polgarus Studios my one stop production shop, but more personally to Graeme Hague for copy editing, Stephanie Parent for your kindness and attention to detail in proofing the manuscript, and to Jason Anderson for formatting. Glendon Haddix of Streetlight Graphics turned the ebook cover into an awesome print one. Martin Stiff of Amazing15, you always manage to interpret my blatherings into the coolest covers imaginable.

Writers are weird. When experts talk about a loss of intimacy due to the internet, I feel they've never researched online writers' groups, which are as strong a community as anything offline. I'm blessed with a mix of online and offline friends that keep me from the Dark Wood. To name a few, I thank the denizens of the Inkbots, Odyssey alum, Swoonreads readers, and the Sunnyside Writers' Group.

I'd be very remiss if I didn't acknowledge the deep debt owed to Jacob and Wilhelm Grimm whose tales I bastardized and twisted to suit my needs to create Milly's book of tales. Specifically, these tales were The Singing Bone, Bearskin, The Ungrateful Son, and The Shroud. Also, credit goes to John Brand who first recorded the Counting Crows rhyme in 1780.

To my wife and daughters, thank you for your ever ready enthusiasm, for your love of fairy tale, you've built my house with the strongest mortar of all, with love and a love of words.

I'd better thank my mom, too, lest she think this book is at all autobiographical! Thank you, Mom! It's not.

Dear Reader, thank you for reading. May you never be afraid to stray from safety's slender path and, when you do, may you find the woods bright and filled with life.

About the Author

Michael is an award winning author who lives in Ottawa, Canada. His graphic novels, novels, and early readers have been published by Rubicon Publishing and distributed by Pearson Education, Scholastic, and Oxford University Press. To learn more about Michael and his projects, visit his website at www.michaelfstewart.com.